SIGHTED FOR SLAUGHTER!

After he had climbed the draw and crept into position behind some rocks, Bischoff raised the rifle's rear sight. The Sharps was cocked and ready to fire. He took a careful rest with his rifle and waited.

He did not have long to wait. Riley soon appeared. But he was still out of sure range. Bischoff aligned his sights on Riley's chest and waited.

Just as a watched wild animal senses danger and becomes uneasy, Riley began feeling apprehensive. He stopped beside a large serviceberry bush. Raising his field glasses he carefully studied the area ahead. Finding nothing, he clucked to his horse and moved forward.

As Riley advanced, Bischoff's finger tightened on his trigger. He could hold dead on now and Riley would be finished when he hit the ground. . . .

RILEY'S
LAST HUNT

Frank Calkins

BALLANTINE BOOKS • NEW YORK

Library of Congress Catalog Card Number: 85-25212

ISBN 0-345-34465-0

This edition published by arrangement with Doubleday and Company, Inc.

Manufactured in the United States of America

First Ballantine Books Edition: May 1987

CHAPTER ONE

T HEL RILEY LIFTED THE BIG WATCH FROM HIS VEST pocket and studied it. He wondered if he was too early. It was 7:30 on the morning of September 2, 1887. The place was the Union Pacific Railroad siding at Rawlins, Wyoming Territory. Riley was here to meet the two big game hunters he was guiding that fall.

He put away his watch and looked across the tracks to where a single passenger car stood gleaming in the sunshine. Riley had never seen one like it. "Private Varnish," the trainmen called them. They were luxurious cars custom-built for America's richest citizens. This car was painted dark green with red trim around the windows and doors. The observation platform had polished brass railings and easy chairs to sit on. In earlier years playboys had shot buffalo from such platforms.

As Riley began to climb the steel steps leading to the car's platform a man opened the door. He was big with a short,

1

grizzled beard and neatly trimmed hair that was thinning on top.

"Riley?" the man asked.

"The same," said Riley smiling. "You must be Henry Marston."

"Indeed!" Marston gave Riley's hand a hearty shake, then led him onto the platform. "Had your breakfast?" asked Marston.

"Yes, sir. We're camped with your outfit a mile from here. I ate before daylight." Thel Riley was just under six feet with a horseman's trim hips and flat belly. He was in his early forties with flecks of gray in his sandy hair. His face showed both his years and his life in the outdoors.

Riley carefully removed his hat as Marston led him into the car. The soft interior lighting gave added elegance to the cherrywood paneling. The richly upholstered furniture almost dripped with fringe and heavy brocades. Thel thought this sure beat the cattle trains he used to ride to Chicago.

Marston invited the guide to sit down at a walnut table with matching chairs, and pulled a heavy golden cord hanging down the wall.

A Negro in white jacket and trousers appeared. "Yes, sir?"

"We'll have coffee," said Marston.

The Negro nodded and disappeared.

"Well, Riley," Marston smiled, "what are my son's chances of killing a grizzly bear?"

Thel Riley was one of the best hunting guides in the Territory. Every season his services were booked by sportsmen who came from all over America. He replied, "Good. With any luck, I can show you both big silvertips."

Marston nodded. "You received my letter of instruction?"

"Yes, sir." Marston's letter had read, in part, "I fought at Gettysburg. I found that for all its horrors, the war made men. My son needs some of that backbone, I have been too generous and spoiled him.

"Riley, show us your West—fang and claw, tooth and

nail. Show my son real danger, a vicious enemy that would eagerly kill him."

Riley winced. "Mr. Marston, my first job is to see you don't get hurt. Maybe your boy will find himself once he's faced a grizzly and shot a moose. There's really no tellin' what two months in the mountains will do for a man."

It was not the answer Marston had wanted. But his frown soon faded and he said, "Eugene is all I have. His mother died when he was five." Marston shook his head. "I've tried everything: preachers, doctors, even a spiritualist. But my son is a weakling. He is also a liar and an accomplished fake."

It was now Riley's turn to frown. He was a guide, not a nanny for spoiled rich boys. But he said to Marston, "Wyoming is make or break. Turn your son loose and see what happens."

Neither man could then realize how prophetic these words would become. They began to discuss the coming hunt. Riley's client was an experienced hunter. Marston had shot a number of white-tailed deer. He had also taken a moose in Maine and caribou in Newfoundland. Now, before they were gone forever, he wanted to hunt the big game animals of the American West.

Riley named them: mule deer, pronghorn antelope, and bull elk that might weigh a thousand pounds on the hoof. The Wyoming moose was larger still. There was always the chance of taking wolves or a mountain lion. Bighorn sheep were plentiful in the Gros Ventre Mountains. If they were very lucky they might find a rogue bull buffalo south of the Yellowstone. In that same region ranged the king—*Ursus horribilis*, the horrible bear. The grizzly bear was the West's most dangerous animal. The great bear with the flash-fire temper had been killing and mangling men for a thousand years.

"By George!" Marston exclaimed, "This should be the hunt of a lifetime! I wish Eugene were here. He left just before you arrived. Said he wanted to look the town over."

Riley sipped his coffee. "Then he'll be back soon. There's not much of Rawlins to look over."

No sooner had he spoken than the car door opened and a tall, good-looking young man entered. At first glance he did not fit the description his father had given to Riley. Eugene Marston had curly blond hair and a thick mustache that drooped over his mouth.

He was wearing a light canvas jacket and leggings to match. It was almost painful for Riley to look at Eugene's hat. It was made of canvas and matched his clothes. The brim was stitched for firmness, allowing the wearer to turn it either up or down. Either way, it made the wearer look like the greenest dude west of St. Louis.

Riley shook hands with young Marston. It was a soft hand, thinskinned like a woman's. Nevertheless Thel found strength in its grip.

Eugene said, "I saw something happen in front of a saloon that I can hardly believe."

Henry Marston interrupted, "You mean Eugene Marston was *outside* a saloon?"

Young Marston flushed but ignored the jibe. "There were some rough-looking men lounging on the porch and passing a bottle around. I guess they were cowboys."

Eugene described what he had seen. A small group of people, obviously foreigners, had approached the saloon. As the group passed, one of the cowboys hooked the toe of his boot in the hem of a peasant girl's skirts.

"Whoee!" he cried, "you hunkies could roost turkeys under all them skirts!" With that he kicked the girl's skirts high above her waist. Nothing was exposed but some gray-looking long underwear, but the girl shrieked all the same.

A young man in her group saw what happened and swung a clumsy punch at the cowboy. It bounced off the man's shoulder, but he immediately rushed the immigrant, tackling him at the waist and driving him over backward into the dusty street. Instantly the red-faced cowboy was astride the immigrant's chest and pounding the man's face with his fists.

His companions cheered him on, "Take it to him, Bob! Teach that Hunky a lesson!"

As Bob's punches rained down, one of his companions

broke the bottom out of a bottle. He put the neck of the broken bottle in Bob's hand saying, "Here, pard, earmark the son of a bitch."

Needing no more encouragement, Bob grabbed the immigrant's hair and twisted his head to one side. Then he ground the bottle's jagged bottom into the side of the man's face.

At this the immigrant's stunned companions reacted, rushing at Bob. But they stopped short when Bob's friends stepped in front of them with drawn revolvers.

H.B. Marston stared at his son. "Eugene, you actually saw this?"

"Yes. It was just up the street not fifteen minutes ago."

Thel Riley said, "He saw it. The railroad brings trainloads of them Hunkys out here every day. They're all carryin' big blue-and-gold booklets telling about free land out West. But this is range land. The stock growers don't want a lot of foreigners cuttin' up the creek bottoms, tryin' to make farms."

"I can understand that," said Henry Marston. "Many of us have petitioned Congress to regulate these foreigners, especially the Orientals. But a man should be able to walk down a street in the United States without being set upon and disfigured."

He asked Eugene, "How could you stand by and allow this to happen?"

"It's easy if the man standing beside you has a derringer pressed against your liver." Eugene flushed as he spoke.

Riley broke in, "I'd say Eugene done the best thing. Some of these locals are just as quick to put it to an Easterner as they are to a Bohunk."

"Well," said Marston, "I guess this is what we came West to find. I just didn't expect it to be so brutal."

Riley said, "We're in hard times out here. Tempers are short. But wait till we get up to Fort Washakie. You may see an Indian wearin' his enemies' fingers on a cord around his neck."

"My God," said Marston.

"Best we get your outfits together," said Riley. "I'd like

to see some of those fine-lookin' guns in your case." Riley indicated a glass-fronted cabinet set against one wall.

"Yes, indeed." Marston took a key from his pocket. He unlocked the cabinet, then swung open the double doors. "Look 'em over, Riley, and suggest the ones you think we should take."

The guide shook his head in wonderment. Standing racked before him in red velvet brackets were twenty of the finest sporting arms in America. There were Winchester, Remington, and Sharps rifles flanked by magnificent English-made double- and single-bore shotguns. Displayed in fitted cases on the bottom of the cabinet were engraved Colt and Smith & Wesson revolvers.

"Go ahead," said Marston taking a long-barreled Winchester single-shot from the rack and pressing it into Riley's hands. "That's a .50/110 Express. T.G. Bennett up at the Winchester works says it's perfect for elk."

"I reckon," said Thel throwing the rifle to his shoulder then replacing it and taking out a lever-action repeater.

"That's their new 1886 model," said Marston, ".45/70. See how it feels."

Riley put the rifle to his shoulder. The balance was perfect and the stock came to his cheek as if it had been fitted for him. "Well, sir I'd like to take 'em all even if they are too pretty to knock around on a hunting trip."

"That's what they're for," said Marston. "I've owned some of those guns for years. After each shooting season they go to the gunsmith's for a complete refitting. Come home as good as new the next summer."

The three men stood admiring and discussing the weapons for an hour. The love of fine weapons predates civilization. Among the tribes, beautifully crafted stone spear points were handed down through generations. Now a brave lucky enough to own a Springfield or coveted Winchester tied a medicine bundle to the muzzle and paid dearly for brass-headed tacks with which to decorate the stock.

Riley's own rifle, a long-barreled Winchester Model 76 lever action, had been sent to him by a grateful client. It was a good shooter but it was heavy and poorly balanced when compared with these new 1886 Winchesters.

Riley suggested that each of the Marstons take a single-shot in .45 or .50 caliber for long-range precision shooting. And, by all means, each should have an 1886 lever gun for all-around shooting.

"Suit yourselves about handguns," said Riley. "There's not much use for 'em hunting. On the other hand, when you're on horseback and need a weapon fast the revolver's about the best there is."

Accordingly Mr. Marston chose a holstered .44 Smith & Wesson double-action. Eugene selected a Colt .45 single-action revolver. He said, "I'll stop at the saddle shop and get a belt and holster."

Riley muttered and both clients looked at him. He said, "Not my place, maybe; but Gene, better not wear that gun until we're out of town. Some of these toughs will use any excuse to start trouble."

H. B. Marston said, "Saying that *is* your place, Riley. After what Eugene told us there is obviously a bad element in Rawlins. We want to avoid them."

Riley agreed but could not help being amused by Mr. Marston's contradictions. On the one hand he wanted his son to face danger. But on the other he was quick to steer him away from trouble on the streets of Rawlins. To Riley, danger was danger. A man couldn't choose the sort he wanted, like picking an apple off a fruit stand. In his time Riley had learned something: the duller the trip, the better he liked it.

The hunting party was ready to leave the following morning. A wagon would carry the party's supplies as far as Fort Washakie. From there everything would be transferred to pack animals.

For the present, Riley was providing a team and a half-dozen saddle horses. At Fort Washakie, Tyghee, his Sho-shone guide, would be waiting with the necessary additional horses. The team and wagon would be left there.

The Marstons' black servant laid out his employers' equipment in the middle of the car. Riley checked it carefully. Dudes usually brought twice too much stuff. But the Marstons had been well advised. They had warm coats and slickers, sturdy boots, overshoes, and extra pairs of warm gloves. They had light as well as heavy underwear plus warm woolen trousers and others of ligther canvas.

Riley advised, "The only thing you might buy here is a pair of chaps each. They're worth their weight in gold in brush, snow, rain, or plain cold weather."

The Marstons agreed and, leaving the Negro to pack, the three men went to buy some chaps. At the harness shop they found a variety of sizes and types.

Eugene held up a furry pair. "Genuine bearskin," said the clerk hopefully.

"They'll do fine with good cowhide," said Riley. The clerk immediately presented two pair of chaps with shiny conchos and fringe down the sides. Riley nodded approvingly.

Marston tried a pair on. "They're fine," he said.

Eugene immediately refused the leg-hugging, shotgun-style chaps his father had chosen. Instead he took a pair of batwings.

"We can sew your initials on these in block letters," said the clerk. "It's a popular addition."

Eugene hesitated. The clerk urged, "It can be done this afternoon. I'll deliver them myself."

Eugene glared at the expectant clerk. Then he angrily snapped, "No, I don't want to look like the louts in Rawlins!"

There were surprised looks all around. Eugene ignored them. "These fringes and gewgaws are ridiculous!" He slapped the chaps back on the counter and stalked from the store.

The clerk looked at Riley in amazement. Their expressions asked, "Well, what brought *that* on?"

The elder Marston looked pained. He said, "I am sorry. My son has not been himself. We will take the chaps, and please have his initials sewn on them." The clerk figured the bill and Marston paid him.

Out on the sidewalk the two men glanced up and down

the dusty street looking for Eugene. He was not to be seen. Marston shoved his hands deep into his pants pockets. "I expect Eugene has gone off by himself. Walk me back to the railroad siding, will you?"

The pair strode along the uneven board walk, ducking the buckets and boots hanging from the mercantile porches. Occasionally passersby greeted Thel and he nodded and called them by name.

"You seem well acquainted," said Marston.

"I'm back and forth through this country pretty regular. When I first came we were still shipping buffalo hides, not the cattle and sheep you see now."

As the men passed an empty lot separating a saloon and café they saw a group of men formed into a circle. The crowd was in a hubbub.

"What's going on?" Marston asked.

"Fight of some kind," Riley answered. "Some of the boys have been paid off for the season. No work for 'em now and they're restless. They'll match dogs, roosters, badgers, men—anything that'll fight and they can bet on."

"Barbaric," said Marston.

"Want to take a look?"

"Of course not." Marston set his lips in a tight line and prepared to pass on.

Suddenly there was a howl from the circled men. Their ring broke as a body came hurtling from the center. The man fell on his hands and knees and the men roared.

"Get up, Wash! Fight or we'll tar your black butt!" The threats were menacing and the black man stood up, staggering.

A huge bare-chested white man pushed his way through the crowd. He was grinning and doubling up his fists. "Here, Toby, here I am." He beckoned to the Negro to come to him.

Riley recognized him as the town bully. He had been matched with a Negro. It was just the sort of one-sided fight this crowd enjoyed. Riley turned to leave just as Henry Marston shoved past him.

"William!" Marston shouted. "What's the meaning of this? What are you doing here?"

"Oh, God," Riley thought. The black was Marston's servant. He'd probably made the mistake of coming into town alone and these loafers had forced him into a fight. The usual inducement for an unwilling fighter was to show him the castrating blade on a clasp knife.

It had not been many years since Big Nose George Parrotti had met his end in Rawlins. George had tried to break jail and a crowd formed. They attempted to lynch the man but their rope broke. So they shot him to death as he lay in the street. Later a doctor skinned Big Nose George and had a vest and moccasins made from the hide.

This event had encouraged mob rule in Rawlins for several years afterward. Now Marston's gentle butler had become the latest victim.

His employer was oblivious of everything but rescuing his servant. He pushed his way into the midst of the crowd and took William's arm.

"Hey, sport, let the nigger go," someone yelled.

"Stand aside," said Marston raising his hand as if he were royalty. Thel Riley muttered an oath and quietly lifted the Colt from its holster on his hip. He stood with the gun pointed at the ground and hoped he would not have to use it.

The bully pushed forward. "Who do you think you are, you eastern dude cow flop?" The man moved on Marston and the crowd behind him roared with delight.

Marston held his ground, crouching a little. William sidled around behind him. "I warn you," said Marston looking at the advancing bully, "do not come closer."

Riley cocked his revolver. But no one heard it as the bully rushed Marston and the crowd cheered approval. Then something most unexpected happened. The bully threw a roundhouse right that struck Marston's plug hat as its owner ducked.

Riley saw someone grab the hat and kick it over a fence. At the same moment Marston seized the bully's right wrist. He threw his own hip into the pug's hip. Then, with a quick jerk and twist, the bully went flying over Marston's shoulder to land hard on his back.

There was a great thud and a whooshing sound. The bully had had the wind knocked out of him. There was absolute silence as Riley stepped in front of Marston. He did not point his Colt at anyone but held it raised so everyone could see it was cocked.

"Mr. Marston," said Riley, "I think we had better move on."

"Yes, indeed. Come, William, they won't trouble you again."

CHAPTER TWO

B<small>ACK AT THE RAILROAD SIDING</small> R<small>ILEY ASKED</small>, "W<small>HAT</small> kind of throw was that, Mr. Marston?"

"It's jujitsu. I learned it at our athletic club. The members brought a Japanese instructor over. Jujitsu is not only good exercise but affords one the means of defending himself."

Without saying it, Riley wondered how much defense jujitsu would have been if he hadn't shown the angry crowd his revolver. In any case they'd had a good lesson, seeing their best pug flat on his back at the feet of a dude.

Before leaving the train yards that afternoon Riley arranged for two railroad detectives to watch Marston's car that night. And he was relieved to see Eugene come sauntering back to the car as he prepared to leave.

In Riley's opinion the sooner the Marstons were out of Rawlins the better. To that end he returned to their car at daybreak with saddle horses and a team and wagon.

The Marstons' baggage was quickly loaded into the

wagon while the two hunters were put aboard their horses. The party had hardly cleared the train yards when a locomotive backed onto the siding. The private car was coupled to it and taken away. The next time the Marstons would see their luxurious car it would be waiting for them on the Northern Pacific tracks in Montana.

Despite their excitement, the Marstons shivered in their heavy coats. Rawlins lies on the high plains 6,700 feet above sea level. It is cold there almost every morning. And on this day in early September, frost rimed the yellowed grasses.

The horses moved easily, their heads bobbing rhythmically. In the brisk, clear air of a Wyoming September men and beasts are at their best. People said Wyoming didn't get much of the Lord's good weather but what He sent was the best He had.

Even the man driving the wagon, a sour apple called Ossie Adams, could not find fault with the morning. Adams was about the age of Henry Marston but looked a decade older. For years he had been Riley's combination cook, wrangler, and packer. Their first hunt together had been for buffalo. The next year they made their last hunt for bison. The great herd had disappeared in the twinkling of an eye, or so it seemed.

Riley had learned to like the older man. But it had been difficult because Ossie's personality made friendship difficult. Once Thel asked him why he always expected the worst.

"Because," Adams explained, "that way I'm never disappointed."

Thel and his hunters soon drew far ahead of the rumbling wagon. Traveling alone did not bother Adams. He had driven this old road many times before. At midmorning he noticed four horsemen overtaking him.

The men rode at an easy lope, the miles rolling away under their horses' hooves. One of the riders called Ossie by name. He replied with a wave.

"Where you headin'?"

"Jackson's Hole and the Yellowstone," called Ossie. "Huntin' two dudes all fall."

The men smiled and waved, passing on quickly and leaving a thin veil of dust trailing behind. They were out of work. The past winter of 1886–87 had decimated many cow outfits. Without cows there were no jobs for cowboys. These fellows were like scores of others: riding, hoping to find work but finding none, riding on. Only the good humor of many of the drifters kept their situation from becoming tragic. Others became angry, and then dangerous men.

As the riders overtook Riley and the Marstons they halooed. Riley waved, his arm stopping for an instant when he recognized two faces from the Rawlins fight crowd.

"Hi, Riley!" a man called. He was a big, rough-looking fellow Riley recognized as Lem Bischoff.

"Hi, yourself," said Riley.

Bischoff rode abreast. "You boys be feelin' pretty good about yourselves today?"

"Tryin' to." Riley felt his stomach tightening.

"Our man, the one that dude throwed, busted his collarbone. He worked in the railroad shops but now he's out of a job."

Marston glared but said nothing. Riley could best handle this.

Thel said, "He should of thought about that before he picked on the nigger."

At the word "nigger" Marston bridled. William had served him for twenty years and he was no "nigger." Riley would be corrected later.

Bischoff took no exception to that. He yelled, "What's our man's wife and kids gonna do with him off work and no pay comin' in?"

Eugene, who had remained silent now, turned in his saddle and looked at his father.

"Don't worry, Eugene," said Marston quietly. "I'll send the lady a check from Fort Washakie."

Eugene nodded. The cowboys were pulling away. At Bischoff's lead they spurred their horses while raising their middle fingers and making derisive noises with their lips. Marston turned crimson and Riley's back stiffened with anger. For his part, Eugene stifled a laugh and turned away so his father could not see his grin. As the four horsemen loped away they could be heard yelling and laughing.

"A bad lot," said Marston.

"Nothing the country would miss," agreed Riley.

Eugene Marston looked at Riley's "country." Even in the golden sunshine it was bleak. Rolling sage plains dotted with rocky, treeless buttes.

The sage looked withered, as if blasted with a gigantic shotgun. Riley said it was done by sheep. Gypsy sheep bands, each one numbering in the thousands, nibbled relentlessly across these lands. Only in summer when the herds were driven into the mountains was there any respite for the range.

There was no game, only the occasional raven or hawk circling high above. Eugene was bored. From Riley's descriptions he had expected to see vast herds of pronghorn antelope and endless flocks of sage hens when they left Rawlins.

Eugene thought of the East and particularly Boston with its brisk fall weather and many fine restaurants. In his mind's eye he saw the Salt House with its delicious smells and snowy tablecloths. He remembered red mahogany woodwork that reflected the crystal lamps overhead. He saw himself in the Belgian mirrors behind the bar. The bartenders wore white jackets and black ties. They always called you "sir" even when you were so drunk they had to lift you into a cab at closing time.

Eugene turned his horse from the road and into a gully thick with greasewood. As he left he said, "Nature calls." His father nodded.

In the gully Eugene dismounted, placing his horse between himself and his father. Assuming himself hidden, he reached inside his coat and withdrew a pint bottle. The whiskey burned as it ran down Eugene's parched throat. He welcomed the discomfort, for even as the alcohol burned it began spreading its warmth throughout his body. He took another drink before returning the pint to his pocket.

His horse looked back as Eugene prepared to mount. "Sorry, old man, you're too old to run but too young to drink." Then, smiling at his own joke, Eugene mounted and trotted his horse from the gulley.

Ossie Adams sat hunched on the wagon seat. A knowing smile played across his lips. He had seen young Marston in the gulley. The dude had been careful to hide from his father. But in doing so he had faced the approaching wagon.

"That little man takes a big drink," thought Adams. And then he felt the swirl of desire become anger at the thought of Eugene's solitary drinking. He shook that off by remembering the whirlwind days after the Civil War. Days and a war he hardly remembered.

All he remembered was blearily looking up one morning to see Thel Riley standing over him. He was a buffalo hunter then: big shoulders and chest and hands large enough to strangle a fence post. All Riley had said was, "Don't drink."

"I won't," replied Adams.

With that Riley shoved the older man onto the seat of his hunting wagon and put the reins into his hands. "You're my cook and skinner. Keep your word and you'll share in the take. Break it and I'll dump you out on the plains like you was just another buffalo chip."

The next weeks were agony for Adams. Some nights he had wanted to kill Riley. And then the man would come up to him out of the darkness and hand him a steaming mug of coffee with plenty of sugar. Even held in both hands, the cup shook and rattled against his teeth. Sometimes the coffee soothed the beast raging inside him. Other times he just vomited and went back to bed feeling worse than ever.

But he made that hunt. When he and Riley returned to the railroad siding with the wagon piled high with hides, Ossie was not a new man. But he was much better than he had been. He'd long since stopped passing blood and his teeth no longer ached and wiggled in his gums.

Riley had paid him five hundred dollars. Ossie Adams boarded the next passenger train going east. He got so drunk that the conductor threw him off in Omaha.

When Thel Riley found him in jail a few weeks later Ossie cried. He said, "I spent all my damn money, Thel. What the hell got into me?"

"The marshal says you made quite a reputation."

"I did?"

"You're well known in every dance house and deadfall in the territory."

"I am?" Ossie grinned foolishly.

"You bet. Not many horses can drink through their cruppers."

Ossie's grin faded and Thel gave him a permanent job. Riley explained it saying, "He's a grumpy old pelter but he owns the best sourdough start in the Territory. Can't lose that."

In this way a relationship developed that was based on one man trusting another and each trusting himself. It was better than a handshake partnership and infinitely superior to the ones the lawyers wrote out and sold for ten dollars each.

Henry Marston was not interested in the old derelict driving Riley's wagon. Men like that littered America's streets and he despised them. Perhaps his hatred was so intense because he feared Eugene might join these men.

But today, Marston was pleased to note, Eugene was sober. Mr. Marston had been careful to ensure that no alcohol accompanied their caravan. And with no saloons in the wilderness to tempt him, Eugene would have to stay sober.

The rutted wagon road went up a dugway. Riley paused at the top to wait for the wagon and to examine the area through his field glasses.

Something caught his eye and he stepped down from his fidgeting horse to study it more carefully. In a moment he said, "There's a fine buck antelope on top of that ridge."

"Where?" asked Henry Marston excitedly.

Riley pointed. "Over yonder a couple of miles. On the ridge where those two junipers stand side by side."

Marston also dismounted and, using his own field glasses, eventually saw the antelope. "What do you think?" he asked Riley.

"I think we should make a try for him. He's a big old buck. Those horns would look good on your wall."

Eugene insisted that his father make the stalk, saying, "It's your trip."

"It's *our* hunting trip, Eugene. But we should make sure to take the first trophy. All right, I'll go with Riley."

It was quickly agreed that Ossie and Eugene would continue on to a campsite while H.B. and his guide stalked the antelope.

Riley saw the eagerness in Marston's expression and cautioned, "This may take time. That buck has been watching us. He sees better with his naked eye than we do with field glasses." And because the pronghorn can outrun anything on four legs, it was necessary to make the stalk while keeping out of his sight. This was accomplished by traveling in the bottoms of the many intervening swales and draws.

To give Marston a fair shot, Riley would have to get him within a hundred and fifty yards of the antelope; a hundred yards would be even better. Marston understood that Riley was leading a skillful stalk. They had come from two miles to within a few hundred yards without spooking the buck. When they reached some shaggy junipers they tied the horses and continued on foot.

Riley stalked with a mental picture of the two of them working up a draw in relation to the antelope on the ridge. As the distance closed, the hunters' stealth increased. When the chance for a look-see from behind some sagebrush presented itself, Riley took it. He crawled up the side of the draw on his stomach.

The buck stood on the ridge and stared at the sagebrush shielding Riley. He had seen a movement, not the man, and he was curious as well as watchful. It was the best buck Riley had stalked in several seasons. The horns would measure twenty inches. Riley looked away from the antelope. He believed it made an animal nervous to stare at it.

Marston came forward at Riley's signal. The older man was in good condition but the excitement had made him red-faced and short of breath. He crawled into position on his stomach.

"See him?" Riley whispered.

"No—uh, yes, I see him." Marston carefully pushed the barrel of his Winchester repeater through the sage and took aim. The buck stood broadside to them one hundred yards distant.

"Damn!" Marston grunted. He had forgotten to lever a cartridge into the rifle barrel. As he did so there was a click and the muted clatter of a brass shell entering the breech. At the sound the antelope threw up his head and whirled, his rump patch flaring white.

Marston fired. The antelope sprang from the ridge, moving with tremendous speed. Riley jumped to his feet and fired offhand just as the buck disappeared into the next ravine. Marston's hasty shot had broken one of the buck's forelegs. Riley's shot flew a fraction too high. Later they found the clipped hair where the slug had grazed the buck across the withers.

"Now what?" asked Marston.

"He's damned scared now and hurtin', too. I'll go get the horses. You sit here and watch." Riley hated wounding game, but it happened. Dudes got excited and even the best shots sometimes just jerked the trigger and hoped.

Marston was waiting when Riley returned with the horses. He said, "I don't know what went wrong. I had a perfect bead on him. In fact I was damned angry when you fired. I expected him to drop within fifty yards." Marston mounted his horse.

"No sir, I never shoot unless I know a critter is wounded.

That buck can go all day on three legs. But we have a chance. Did you see him again?"

Marston had seen the buck emerge from a fold in the rolling hills and limp across an open ridge. Riley mentally marked the location Marston had given him, then led the way there.

Dismounting on the ridge, Riley began looking for tracks. There would be little blood from a broken foreleg. To his credit, Marston hadn't just damned his bad luck and refused to track the buck as some hunters would have done.

Riley tracked from the saddle and at 4 P.M. found the buck. He was lying on the point of a low ridge a mile away. There was no cover and no convenient draw to sneak up and shoot from. Riley doubted the buck would allow them within five hundred yards before getting up and limping away.

"It looks hopeless," said Marston.

"Not quite. Come on." Riley rode off the ridge they were on and stopped beside a clump of junipers. He dismounted and tied his horse.

"We'll try something Tyghee showed me," said Riley. As he explained the strategy, Marston shook his head but agreed to try.

When the men emerged from behind the junipers, Riley was on foot with Marston walking behind and leading his horse. Riley was bent double at the waist. Marston bent, too, holding one arm out straight and gripping Riley's hip pocket while leading his horse with the other. The idea was to resemble two horses, one following the other.

They saw the buck watching them but he did not get up. The men continued to advance, moving through the low sage toward a point below the wounded buck.

The late afternoon sun was hot on their backs and both men began to ache from walking stooped over. As they came within four hundred yards of the antelope, Riley sensed it was about to bolt.

He whispered, "I'm going to stop in that high sage just

ahead. When I do, you drop back beside your horse and keep walking."

Riley told Marston to keep himself hidden from the antelope by staying behind his horse. When Marston reached the end of the ridge on which the buck lay, he was to turn up the next draw. "When you think you're abreast of the buck, Indian up the ridge and shoot him. I'll try to hold his attention."

When they reached the patch of sage Riley had chosen, he dropped down beside it. Marston walked ahead as instructed. Riley rolled over on his back and began kicking his feet in the air. Riley was hidden by the sage and all the buck could see were his feet. The buck's attention alternated between Riley's rotating feet and Marston's departing horse.

Lowering his feet, Riley broke a stick from a sagebrush and tied his red bandana to it. He raised the cloth and began waving it slowly to and fro. The buck appeared to forget Marston and begin concentrating on the tantalizing bandana. The red cloth fluttered, rising and falling on the soft wind currents.

Come on, Riley thought, *keep lookin'*. He lowered the flag and again kicked his booted feet in the air.

Suddenly, but with obvious effort, the buck stood up. His dark brow, cheeks and black horns stood out starkly against the sky. The animal could not take his eyes off that puzzling object in the sage. He hobbled a few steps toward Riley. Riley waved the bandana flag. The antelope came nearer. The flag fluttered back and forth, back and forth hypnotically. The buck, with ears forward and watching intently, limped toward Riley.

He never saw the movement on the adjacent rise of ground. Riley saw a spear of yellow flame. The boom rolled across the silent hills long after the antelope had fallen. Riley sprang to his feet. They had done it!

The guide was jubilant. He could not explain it, but when a stalk ended and the game fell to a single, well-placed shot he brimmed over with the joy of satisfaction.

It was a fine buck. The black pronged horns had sharp ivory tips and were easily twenty inches long.

"Boss, that was a good shot."

Marston beamed. "Yes, sir, damn me if it wasn't!" He was still bubbling when Thel left to fetch his horse.

When Riley returned he dressed the buck in fading light. The guide looked to the west and set his mental compass in the direction he expected to find camp. Then he loaded the buck across his saddle. He tied the head behind the cantle and lashed the legs to the cinch rings.

To Marston he said, "We'll take a line west. With me walkin' it'll be three hours before we find Ossie and your son."

When he at last saw a campfire twinkling in the distance, Thel called out. There was an answering shout. As the two hunters approached the camp their weariness was replaced by happy pride.

"Hey Ossie!"

"Yoo!" Shadowy figures moved in the firelight. A lantern appeared. Coming closer, Thel recognized Ossie Adams.

"Mr. Marston got a fine buck. Biggest one I . . ." Riley's voice trailed off. He sensed that something was wrong in camp.

"We had company," said Ossie. "Those four riders showed up 'bout the time we had staked the horses and throwed the bedrolls down."

"What happened?" Riley asked, his voice sharp.

"Bastard roped me," said Ossie.

"Where is Eugene?" Marston interrupted.

"He's in bed, Mr. Marston. Your boy saved me a draggin'."

When the cowboy roped Ossie, Eugene had leaped in to help the older man. He grabbed the taut lariat and gave it a tremendous jerk. Eugene not only knocked Ossie down but jerked the roper's saddle sideways. To avoid being spilled, the man threw off his dally and jumped from his horse. He charged Eugene with his fists flailing.

Eugene dodged, then struck the man with a long billet of firewood from the pile. The cowboy went down and when he tried to rise he found Ossie covering them all with a double-barreled shotgun.

Holding the shotgun with one hand, Ossie pulled the noose from around his waist and stepped free of it. "That's enough," he panted. "You boys have had your fun. Call it even and get out of here."

Ossie's would-be tormentor stumbled to his horse, reset the saddle, and mounted. "Next time, dude, you'll have to fight fair. You won't use no club on a man!"

Eugene did not reply but, still holding the heavy stick he'd used as a weapon, stood watching the four cowboys.

Ossie said, "There ain't gonna be a next time. Now, git!"

Bischoff, the leader, turned his horse slowly, reining him tightly to make a little show. Then he loosened the reins and the horse stepped prettily around the campsite. Bischoff swung his mount again, spurred him hard, and the horse leaped away into the darkness. It was a calculated display of contempt. Adams had seen Indians do it to taunt their enemies.

But he let it pass; it didn't matter. The men had left and that was all they wanted, nothing more.

"Thanks, mister," said Adams. "I'm gettin' too old to be jobbed by kids half my age."

Young Marston threw down the stick. "No matter. My father would have broken his collarbone."

"We'll have supper soon," said Ossie.

Marston said, "I'm too tired to eat." He unfastened the straps binding his bedroll. Reaching inside the roll, he pulled out a quart bottle. Adams heard the squeak and pop of a cork. He smelled the biting aroma of whiskey.

"Care for a drink?" Eugene asked.

Ossie took a step forward. His old companion stood before him again, calling, beckoning, offering warmth and oblivion.

Then Ossie stopped. "No, sir, I better not. Fact is I been

a booze fighter . . ." Ossie paused, embarrassed to have said it.

Marston replied, "Never mind. Just remembered, there are more old drunks than old doctors. Think about it."

"Yes, sir." Ossie scratched his head and turned back to his cooking.

CHAPTER THREE

After listening to Ossie's report, Henry Marston was more eager than ever to see his son. "Where is Eugene? I want to see that boy!" His voice was bursting with paternal pride.

"Eugene!" he called, trying to locate his son in the flickering firelight.

Ossie said, "He turned in, over by the wagon." Ossie looked up from his pots and pans to give Riley a meaningful stare.

Marston hastened to the wagon. Initially his voice was low and filled with warmth. Then Eugene replied, his voice also low but sounding cross.

"Damn!" Marston spat out the word. In the dim light Riley saw him lunge at Eugene. When he stepped back, there was a bottle in his hand. He smashed it against the wagon's iron tire.

Riley said nothing when Marston came striding angrily back to the fire.

Marston said, "He's drunk! Here, in the space of an hour, the boy shows some grit. And now he's drunk! Adams, did you give him that bottle?"

"No, sir." Ossie sounded wounded.

"He's found some. I thought we made sure there was no liquor anywhere in this camp."

"I guess there isn't now, Mr. Marston." Thel took his distraught client's arm. "C'mon, let's eat. Ossie, you should have seen the shot Mr. Marston made on that buck . . ."

But try as he would, Thel Riley could not relieve the somber mood. Later, sitting alone with his coffee and thoughts, he wondered why some people believed a hunting trip would solve their problems. Marston appeared to think a grizzly bear and buffalo could miraculously jolt Eugene into taking the pledge.

Thel decided he could produce the animals, but the Marstons would have to solve their problems themselves. He turned in, feeling a pang of regret that a bottle of whiskey could make everyone forget a fine buck antelope.

In the morning Riley and Ossie were busy with camp chores and the horses when the Marstons finally rolled out. While Adams cooked breakfast Thel watered the horses and harnessed the team. Next he measured oats into two nose bags and hung them on the draft animals. Looking at the contented animals, Thel was reminded of the old remark: A hunting guide had the best job in the world if he just didn't have to contend with hunters.

After breakfast the party would be riding toward the lumpish Green Mountains lying to the north. There was a good chance of finding more antelope and perhaps some deer en route. Riley liked to blood his guests on harmless creatures before pitting them against grizzly bears and other potentially dangerous game.

Henry Marston was up now. He stumped over to the basin of hot water Ossie set out for him. He was obviously sore from his unaccustomed exertions. His graying hair rose in tangled wisps. Thel wondered how well he had slept.

Eugene sat up in his blankets. His eyes looked watery and

bloodshot. A commiserating Ossie handed him a steaming mug of coffee.

"Serving breakfast in bed?" asked Eugene.

"Nope, and don't expect coffee very often. Thel figures you and him will hunt antelope today. Wants you to get ready."

Young Marston sipped the hot coffee and gingerly smoothed his touseled hair. "Ossie, if I shot a rifle this morning my head would come off. You haven't got a little something . . ?"

"Sorry, you know the orders. We're all Sons of Temperance on this hunt." Ossie stepped to the campfire and returned with the coffeepot.

As he refilled Eugene's cup he caught the unmistakable aroma of liquor. "Why, that scamp," he thought. "Hittin' me up for a drink when he had a bottle all the time." If Ossie knew anything about a man with a thirst, and he did, there were bottles stashed all through the duffel.

But, whatever the source of his strength, Eugene Marston was ready to ride after breakfast. H.B. Marston did not protest when he was asked to ride with Ossie and the wagon. It would give his sore muscles a chance to recuperate.

Thel moved his big gelding out briskly. He and Eugene would make a wide circle through the country east of them and rendezvous with the wagon at noon.

The men rode side by side. Eugene did not scan the horizon for game the way his father did. Riley didn't care. He was paid to locate the game. But he drew the line at shooting animals for sports who preferred to stay in camp with their drinks and cards.

Eugene had few comments. That suited his guide, who concentrated on looking for game. It was the antelopes' rutting season and there was likely to be a good-sized buck in any herd they saw.

Riley enjoyed watching a buck antelope herding his does. The bucks could circle and double back faster amd more surely than the best cow pony. Few does, even if they truly wanted to, could slip off and outrun a determined buck. If a doe tried it, the buck would drop his head then fly like the wind to overtake her and turn her back into his herd. If an intruding younger buck appeared, he would be run off. Riley had seen a herd buck chase a competitor five miles. Sometimes the bucks fought, and on rare occasions one buck killed the other.

When Riley thought about the courtship of the antelope he was reminded of his cow-punching days on the Sweetwater. There were lots of antelope in the area. He was riding for the pioneer rancher Ben Amerall, whose far-flung herds seemed to be everywhere in those days. But when you rode for Ben you didn't eat beef, not with so many antelope around.

When he hunted, Thel had sometimes taken Beatrice Dane with him. Bea was a tawny-haired beauty who lived with her parents in South Pass City. On Sunday afternoons she rode out with Thel and made him feel he was the only man in the Territory. They fished in the stream and shot deer, antelope, and sage grouse in the surrounding meadows. Bea prepared their picnic lunches and sometimes let Thel kiss her as they sat together beside the river.

But Bea had a frustrating quality—a kind of distant self that never let Thel come too close. It had seemed so simple to Thel. He wanted to take up ranching. And he wanted Bea to be his wife and raise their kids in the house he would build for her.

Bea must have known Thel was desperately in love with her, but her responses to him ran hot and cold. She said she loved Wyoming and the times they had together on the Sweetwater. And then she would tell him of Eastern cities and the handsome young men there who took her to parties and fancy balls. Riley berated himself for lack of knowledge of such things. And he was panicked by the knowledge that Bea had another serious suitor, a handsome young Army lieutenant from Fort Stambaugh.

One day when Bea came for her ride with Thel she was wearing a beautiful gold locket around her neck. Thel admired it. "That sure is a pretty thing, Bea. Where did you get it?"

"Harold gave it to me. He ordered it from Tiffany's in New York."

Thel's heart sank into his boots. "Harold" was the young lieutenant. "Oh," said Thel. Bea showed him how the monogram "B" had been engraved on the locket. But Thel could not look at it. He would have liked to take it and hurl it into the river.

The couple rode silently for a long time. Finally Bea reached over and put her hand on Thel's arm. "What's the matter, Thel? You've hardly said a word."

Her touch was so gentle and her voice so warm that Thel felt even more miserable for behaving so badly. He did not know what to do. He even thought of killing the young officer.

That chance almost came a few weeks later. Thel was hunting for cows when a small detachment of cavalry trotted up to him. Leading it was Bea's young lieutenant, Harold Woods.

Accompanying Woods was a burly sergeant with six troopers. They stopped and Woods smiled. "You're Thel Riley, aren't you?"

"Yeah," Riley could find nothing to say.

"How are your cattle doing?"

"Not bad, only it'd be nice if you soldier boys would stop the Injuns from stealin' 'em."

Woods's smile faded. "Beatrice mentioned you were herding cattle in these meadows. You know, by treaty the Indians have a right to hunt here. If you have trouble with them come to the fort and report it."

"If I did, the whole herd would be gone by the time I got back." Riley hated this neatly uniformed young officer with his smooth talk and smoother ways.

Woods stiffened and his voice hardened. "I didn't know herding cattle was so difficult. From what I've seen, the only requirements are a thick butt and a thicker head."

With that Riley sprang from his saddle, clawing at the officer, pulling him from his horse and punching him at the same time. Woods fought back. His heavy leather glove split Riley's lip with one punch.

Before Thel could retaliate, four troopers dived on him, knocking him to the ground. Woods stepped back and let his sergeant replace him. The troopers hauled Riley to his feet while the sergeant waded in, his big fists pounding Riley's belly and ribs. He kicked at the sergeant, who sidestepped and pumped three sledgehammer blows into Riley's kidneys. Then the sergeant stepped back and nodded. The troopers let Riley fall on his face.

Riley stayed close to the cow camp until his bruises healed. When he finally returned to South Pass City it was to learn that Bea and Lieutenant Woods had left Wyoming together. The couple planned to be married at his parents' home in Maryland. Riley knew he would never see Bea again—not the Bea he had known and loved beside the Sweetwater.

"What's that?" Eugene Marston's question returned Riley to the present.

"Sage chickens," said Riley. Ahead in the low sage were scores of large gray birds. Some were scurrying along excitedly, while others stalked majestically across the slope before them.

"Think you could shoot the heads off a couple with your Winchester?" Riley asked.

"They're too far," said Marston.

"We'll get closer. The young ones are about as good eating as anything that flies." Riley pulled his rifle from the scabbard beneath his leg. Then, balancing the rifle across his lap, the guide rode forward. Eugene followed, curious.

The birds grew nervous and several flushed, their big wings flapping noisily. Riley ignored them. Most of the birds had stayed on the ground. The men rode along the edge of the flock until he and Eugene were within easy range of dozens of birds.

"Gene," said Thel, "get down. Now take a rest and try to hit 'em in the neck or head. A high shot in the back won't spoil much meat, either."

Tying their horses to some thick sagebrush, the men sat down and began shooting. At each of Riley's shots a grouse fluttered then fell, its wings flapping violently. Marston missed most of his shots, and despite Riley's advice he could not readily distinguish tough old roosters from the more tender young birds.

As the men fired, the birds flushed or ran wildly through the sage. Soon most of the flock had either flown or hidden in the sage. Riley flipped his rifle's lever one last time and stood.

"That's plenty. Let's gather up our birds and head for the wagon."

Riley had fired seven shots and killed seven young grouse. Marston's aim had been much less precise. Most of his birds had been blasted into inedible gobs of bloody flesh. He was appalled by the carnage caused by his .45/70.

As the men searched the sage, retrieving their birds, a figure appeared on the skyline. It was a white man, skinny, with long arms and legs jutting from too-short sleeves and pants. He was waving his hat and yelling unintelligibly. He was leading a sway-backed bay horse.

Riley straightened up and regarded the fellow as he approached them.

"Stop!" The man was alternately jerking his horse's halter and waving his arms.

"We're stopped," said Riley, grinning at the ridiculous figure stumbling toward them through the sage.

In his ragged knee-length coat, baggy pants, and seam-split shoes the man resembled a scarecrow. His face was a sunburnt red with deep-set eyes of watery blue. His bristling whiskers had not been trimmed for a week.

He kept babbling long before he was close enough for Riley and Eugene to understand him. "You should of seen what I done! He come again last night. But I put a bullet in him this time. I know it. When I shot he bellered like he'd been burnt."

"Whoa, whoa!" Riley could not help laughing. He had seen dozens like this one, crazy sheepherders. They lived alone with their blatting flocks for so long that a chance to be with fellow humans overwhelmed them. In an attempt to calm the man Riley fished in his shirt pocket and produced the makings.

"Here," he said, "have a smoke and tell us about it."

The sheepherder took the tobacco eagerly. "Thanks," he said, beginning to roll a cigarette. "Name of Viro Pocket. Come from Kentucky." He licked the cigarette then stuck it into his mouth. Riley lit it for him.

"Thanks again. Lost my makin' about a week ago. Won't see the camp tender for a time yet. Wonder could I buy these?"

"Keep 'em," said Riley. "I've got plenty back in camp." Riley in fact smoked very little, carrying tobacco as much for moments like this as for his own enjoyment.

The herder's weathered face broke into a wolfish grin. "Well, sir, that's decent as Sunday afternoon. By the way, I'm Viro Pocket. Now if you could just help me get rid of that bugger . . ."

"Lem Bischoff and his pals have't been hoorawing you, have they?" asked Riley.

"No, no. You're the first white men I've seen in three weeks." Pocket chattered on, "He come in last night and kilt another thirty. Just kilt 'em and jerked the pelts. Didn't hardly eat a one. Now the coyotes and wolves are cleanin' up and just waiting their chance to do me *their* devilment."

Riley held up his hand. "Have you got a bear?"

"Mister, I got the biggest bear goin'. He stood up t'other night and I swear he is eight feet tall." Pocket held up his right hand as if taking an oath.

"You shot this bear?" asked Eugene Marston.

"Yes, sir," Pocket grinned and reached for the battered rifle hanging from his saddle. "Thirty-two, she is. Only a single-shooter, but hard-shootin' and true to two hundred yards for a fact."

Riley looked at the rifle. It was a cheap single-shot breech loader. He marveled that any man could consider himself well armed with such a weapon. A rimfire rifle of dubious accuracy and power. And Pocket had had the nerve to shoot a bear with it!

"You're sure you hit that bear?" asked Riley.

"You bet I hit him. He bawled and rubbed his shoulder

on the ground like a dog does sometimes. Then he left arunnin'."

Riley decided the .32 bullet had indeed struck the bear's shoulder. But he doubted that the slug had penetrated deeply enough to do more than make the bear sore and very mean.

"Tell you what, Viro Pocket," said Riley, "we'll ride over with you now and take a look. I'd like to see this bear's tracks. Maybe we can take him off your hands."

Pocket replied, "I figure that bear should already be dead and lyin' in some draw. But if you was to come and help me find him I'd be obliged."

It was an hour's ride to where Pocket had left his sheep. The herd was bedded for its midday meditations and was watched by two shaggy sheep dogs.

"Wonder you'd leave your sheep with that bear around," said Riley.

"He only comes by night. Not got the guts to come in daylight." Pocket patted his rusty rifle and both Riley and Eugene stifled grins.

Piled in a ravine were the bloody carcasses of the sheep Pocket had lost. A cloud of ravens and squawking magpies rose when the men approached.

Riley dismounted and began searching the ground for tracks. "Here they are," he said pointing to the flat-footed tracks of a bear.

"Grizzly, ain't he? Old Silvertip," said Pocket.

"No, he's not a grizzly," said Riley. "But he's got the biggest track I've seen in five years. Eugene, I think we better go get your dad. This is some bear, even if he is just a black."

After assuring the sheepherder that they would help him, the two hunters rode back to the wagon road. Henry Marston twisted in his saddle as they approached.

Seeing their sage chickens he said, "Got some birds, eh? What about big game?"

Thel smiled, "We located a big bear."

"You don't mean it! A bear? In this God-forsaken country?"

Eugene said, "We met a shepherd whose flock has been

raided. I saw the pile of dead sheep. We promised the man we'd help him."

Henry Marston grinned. Sometimes when he did that Thel thought he resembled an old bruin himself. Marston said, "Of course we want that bear, don't we, Eugene?"

The young man shrugged. "I could get along without it. But the man obviously needs help." Eugene's lack of enthusiasm seemed designed to annoy his father.

Nevertheless their strategy was quickly decided. Ossie was to proceed with the team to their next camping spot. Thel and the Marstons would return to the sheep camp and begin tracking the bear.

As they rode, Thel warned them that any bear was potentially dangerous. An old stock killer with a .32 bullet festering in him must be assumed vicious.

Viro Pocket was moving his sheep when the hunters arrived, and in the process his flock's sharp hooves had obliterated the bear's tracks. It was already late afternoon and Thel cursed the delay caused by having to relocate the bear's tracks.

"Viro," asked Riley, "will either of your dogs hunt?"

"Don't know, never hunted 'em." He whistled the dogs in, then followed Riley on foot while he found the bear's tracks.

The Marstons sat their horses and stayed out of the way. Like most dudes they couldn't track a hog through a foot of fresh snow. But, unlike many dudes, they admitted it.

After finding the bear's spoor, Riley summoned Pocket and his dogs. Thel said, "Scent's pretty cold but let's try." With Pocket's help he pressed the nose of one of the dogs against the bear's print. Immediately the dog began to *ki-yi* and broke away from its master. Ignoring the herder's calls, the yelping canine raced for Pocket's tent and dived in under the flap.

"Guess he's not a bear dog," said the guide with a wry smile.

"Tige here'll do it. He's my best dog." Pocket dragged the dog to the track by the scruff of the neck. The dog had been hanging back. But when his nose was passed over the

bear track it stopped, then plunged into the impression.
Tige's gray muzzle curled into a vicious-looking snarl.
From his throat came an ominous growl.

Riley grinned. "Maybe we got a bear hunter. Viro, put a
rope on your pup. Give him his head and hang on."

For the first half mile Riley had Viro restrain his dog. He
wanted to be sure the animal wouldn't take off on a coyote
track and lead them astray. But every time he checked,
Riley found the dog welded to the bear's trail.

Pocket wanted to return to his sheep, so the dog was
released. He went chasing after the bear with the hunters
loping along behind.

The bear had traveled fast but had stopped occasionally to
roll or rub himself against a large rock. Riley found traces
of dried blood. "He's shot, all right." He showed the
Marstons the bloodstains, saying, "It looks dark; probably a
flesh wound. Keep your eyes open. He could be hidin'
anywhere."

The trail led into a rocky ravine that twisted and turned
amidst brushy overhangs. Riley thought, "This could be it.
If I was a hurt bear I'd lay up in here." He slowed the pace,
not wishing to stumble on the bear unprepared.

Overhead the sky was purpling as the sun set. Long
shadows spread across the draw. At a brushy fissure in the
rocks they found where the bear had denned. Tige set up a
terrific barking and Thel found fresh blood.

"Come on!" he ordered. "Get down and tie your horses.
I'm going to tie the dog here. We don't need him now. The
track's real fresh and we'll go in on foot."

There was a clatter of rifles as cartridges were levered
into gun barrels. Riley led the way with Henry and Eugene
Marston following closely. Riley could hear the hunters'
nervous puffing behind him.

The bear had not left the ravine. He was looking for a
place to hide. And he was choosing a rough location that
grew worse with every yard. The ravine's walls grew
steeper and began closing in on the men. There were
overhanging ledges and huge boulders on every side. The
thick stands of brush could hide a dozen bears.

CHAPTER FOUR

RILEY GLANCED AT THE WESTERN SKY. ANOTHER FIVE minutes of light was all he could hope for. He hated to pull off the bear's trail when they were so close. But he would hate even more to have someone mauled or shot in the poor light. Mr. Marston was at his side, ready, determined. Eugene was lagging behind again and holding his rifle at the grip and resting it on his shoulder. A prudent guide watched his hunters as carefully as he did the game.

Suddenly there was a frantic scrabbling on the rocks behind them. Riley turned, covering the ravine with his rifle. A blurred shape flashed into view. Riley threw his front sight on it and tightened his finger on the trigger.

"Damn! Don't shoot! It's the dog!" He had nearly shot Tige, the sheep dog.

The dog, his tongue lolling, burst past them. "No! Come here!" Riley called.

But the dog paid no heed, bounding ahead and then

leaping over a dark boulder that stood a few steps in front of them. As Tige cleared the boulder there was a furious "Woof!" and a huge black bear stood erect to meet the dog's attack.

"Tige!" yelled Riley. But it was to no avail. The dog landed squarely on the bear's chest, snarling and snapping while the bear roared a furious protest.

Riley aimed his rifle but bear and dog were a blend of battling fury. To shoot now might kill the dog. Marston was aiming, too. But he remained cool, waiting to touch the trigger until the bear was clear in his sights. And it was not clear. The bear swung at the swarming dog, who somehow dodged the lethal blows.

The ravine was in pandemonium. Everyone was yelling at the dog while raising, then lowering his rifle. The bear ws at bay, roaring and fighting for his life. Then came a blow the dog did not dodge. Tige was flung howling into a patch of brush and the bear dropped to all fours. Snarling and with ears flattened against his skull, the bear was about to charge.

"Shoot!" yelled Riley. Immediately there was a burst of flame from Henry Marston's gun muzzle. For some reason Riley glanced at Eugene, who was aiming.

"No!" Riley whirled and with his forearm knocked Eugene's rifle barrel skyward. The gun roared and its heavy slug smacked angrily into the ravine wall. The bear was nearly on Henry Marston when Tige flashed from the brush and seized the bear by the ear. Instantly the bear stopped and grabbed the struggling dog in his forepaws. He was about to crush the dog's head in his jaws when Riley's bullet struck him under the eye.

The bear dropped the dog and fell forward. Henry Marston fired at point-blank range and the bullet smashed the bear's spine between the shoulder blades. There was a last furious growl and the bear lay still. Riley stepped forward and dragged the furious Tige away from the carcass.

The two Marstons stood, rifles at the ready but paralyzed

by the savage violence they had witnessed. Then Eugene sank down on a rock, holding his rifle between his knees.

Even Thel Riley had to take a deep breath before saying, "Men, that was a bear hunt! I don't want 'em any closer than that."

Henry Marston lowered his rifle and carefully removed the live round from the chamber. His hands were shaking. "It happened so fast. I never expected it to happen so fast. That bear almost got me."

Eugene said, "Riley and the dog saved you, Father."

Thel said, "I don't know if the dog helped or not. He did grab the bear's ear. But he might have started the charge by runnin' in ahead the way he did." Riley looked questioningly at the bloodsmeared dog whose tail wagged happily.

Marston said, "I want to buy that dog. Never saw courage like that. He never hesitated. Eugene, you saw it?"

The young man replied, "Yes, Father, I saw it." Then he looked at Riley. Their eyes met and Eugene looked away.

Riley said nothing. It had all happened so fast he could not be sure now exactly what he had seen. But what he *thought* he had seen was Eugene Marston preparing to blow off the back of his father's head. That was why he had knocked Eugene's gun away.

Marston set his rifle aside and began examining the bear. He put his forefinger on the white triangle at the base of the bear's throat. "Here's my shot, centered. It didn't seem to phase him."

Riley glanced at the bloody hole his bullet had made just under the bear's eye. Brain shot, it had to be. Marston's bullet would have killed the bear but too slowly to save the hunter from being mauled.

"Where did you hit him, Eugene?" Marston asked.

"My shot went wild. I didn't have time for another."

Riley sat down and rolled a cigarette. As he smoked, the tension and excitement within him began to subside. Eugene Marston sat across from him shrouded in the gathering dusk. Eugene's features were rigid except for the working of his jaw muscles. The guide would have liked to be able to read his thoughts.

Henry Marston appeared oblivious of everything except the killing of the bear. "Gentlemen," he beamed, his face still flushed with excitement, "that was an *experience*. Riley, do you think we can repeat it with a grizzly? I want Eugene to have the shot next time."

Marston appeared to be overlooking the fact that it was Riley who dropped the bear. A good guide did not lay on charges for added excitement.

Riley said, "Eugene will have a shot. But remember, a grizzly's likely to be bigger and meaner than any black bear. Stopping charges at ten feet is pinching it too fine."

"Of course," Marston replied. "But that was a priceless moment—like being in a battle. I wouldn't have missed it."

Riley had guided hunters who broke and ran when a wild animal charged. A raging bull moose had once knocked him flat and broken his ribs. He did not share H.B. Marston's enthusiasm for the charge.

It was decided to leave the bear where it had fallen and return for the pelt in the morning. Evening was coming on cool and the hair would not slip overnight. Besides, Ossie was alone. They could not be sure Bischoff and his mischievous companions wouldn't make another call.

After recovering the horses and leaving Tige at the sheep camp the men set out for their camp. Eugene brought his horse up beside Riley's. As the two men rode stirrup to stirrup, Riley waited to be questioned about knocking Eugene's rifle aside.

Eugene, however, said nothing about it. From his behavior, the incident might never have happened. He did say, "My father courts danger. He takes risks in business and enjoys sailing when the storm flags are flying. It doesn't matter to him that other people could be hurt."

Thel replied, "That's his business. But hunting out here is dangerous enough without lookin' for trouble. That's one pot I don't stir."

Eugene nodded, then glanced back at his father. The

older man was fifteen yards to the rear and almost invisible in the darkness. Eugene reached inside his coat. Riley heard the faint pop of a cork.

Riley almost said something. Then, thinking better of it, he slapped his reins across his thigh and his horse picked up the pace.

The men rode in silence, each absorbed in his own thoughts. The blue-black sky glowed with the light of a million stars. The coyotes relayed a series of eerie howls that were carried from one ridge to another, then back again.

H.B. Marston sat slumping in his saddle. He was sorely tired. His thoughts were dominated by the image of the bear rising to meet them, and of the fearless Tige dashing forward and attacking the bear. He wondered what it was that made one dog, or man, a hero and another a whining coward. The sheepherder's two dogs looked much alike, yet one yelped at the mere scent of a bear while the other flew at the beast.

Marston thought this fellow Riley was all right. He had stood his ground and shot the bear as calmly as if he'd been firing at a tin can. The fellow was not well educated, but he was personable and wise enough to keep quiet when the conversation turned to a subject he did not understand. Riley's only flaw, Marston decided, was his reluctance to help shape the hunt into the means of making Eugene a man.

Marston stared through the gloom to Eugene, riding hunched in his saddle. He had stood firm during the charge; his father gave him that. The next time, Henry Marston promised himelf, Eugene would not only stand but fire the killing shot. He would never have believed that Eugene might have aimed his rifle at the back of his father's head. Nor would he have considered that Riley might have saved his life twice that afternoon: once from the bear and once from his son.

At that moment Eugene did not hate his father. The gin he had been sipping had spread its mellow warmth throughout his body. The tension and lumpish pain he had felt in the pit of his stomach were gone. Eugene knew they would return but he also knew how to get rid of them.

Eugene considered his father a tyrant. The older man always had an answer for every question. And he offered his solutions without being asked. *No!* Eugene thought. His father's advice gushed out: "Get a job. Sign the pledge. Be a man! 'Much drinking, little thinking.'"

Besides, Eugene thought, *I don't drink nearly as much as Father seems to think. And I can quit any time I want to.*

A night breeze raised in the northern mountains began to sweep across the rolling hills. It carried with it fragments of warmth from the sunbaked foothills amidst gusts of cold from the mountaintops. Eugene turned his face into the breeze. Then he pulled his neck deeper into his coat collar and took a crafty swallow of gin.

It was nearly 10 P.M. when the hunters rode into Ossie's simple camp. The fire had burned low but there was coffee steaming in the big pot, and crusty pieces of sage grouse stayed hot in the Dutch oven. While Thel unsaddled and fed the horses Ossie snatched baked potatoes from the fire's coals.

"Hey, boys," he called, "I've got sage chicken but how about some antelope steaks to go with it?"

Eugene threw himself down beside the fire. "You name it, we'll eat it." He could not remember ever having been so hungry. His father sank down beside him and nodded appreciatively as Ossie handed him a mug of steaming coffee.

"We got our bear," said Henry Marston.

"You mean you got it," said Eugene. "My shot missed."

Thel came and helped himself to a cup of coffee. "We got a big bear, Os. Mr. Marston hit him square in the neck at about fifteen feet. We'll go up early tomorrow and skin him. Maybe the Marstons will want to sleep in, good chance."

Ossie listened with feigned interest. It was part of the job, like listening to the dudes telling hunting yarns he'd heard a hundred times before. "This big buck and that big bear. The cougar on the ledge." The yarns were part fact, part fiction vigorously blended with imagination. And then the tellers would eat and crawl wearily into their sougans. They would be snoring by the time Ossie collected their cups and plates and began to wash them.

"I'll dry," Thel knelt beside Ossie, wiping the utensils and placing them on the clean square of canvas spread on the ground.

"Got a bear, did you?" Ossie asked.

"It was closer than I like. That crazy sheepherder's crazy dog got in the middle of it. He's a gutty whelp. Mr. Marston gave orders to buy him."

"Didn't think you'd want a dog in a huntin' camp." Ossie scraped at the hardened crust in a frying pan.

"I don't. You'll have to help me keep an eye on him. We can't have him runnin' the country and chasing the game away."

"Maybe those Shoshones at Fort Washakie will put him in their stewpot." Ossie clearly felt he had enough duties without adding that of dog watcher.

"Tyghee will stop that," said Riley. He thought of the wiry Indian guide with the lined brown face, who reminded Thel of Sitting Bull with heartburn. He thought, too, of the way that stern Indian expression became a boyish grin when a stalk succeeded and the game was down.

Riley asked, "Do you think we'll be hoorawed again by Bischoff and his friends?"

"Hard tellin'," Ossie replied. "Bischoff and that little partner of his are no good. But the other two aren't bad fellows. They're just on the bum and didn't like bein' showed up by one of our dudes."

In Wyoming, nonresident Easterners or English peers wearing little bitty eyeglasses on their sharp noses often owned the largest ranches. Now the railroads were flooding the country with homesteaders. It would have been surprising for men riding the grub line not to have resented newcomers.

When Ossie turned in that night Thel noticed that he was sleeping with a shotgun. His sympathies may have been with the cowpunchers but his loyalties were to his own outfit.

Thel also turned in with his weapons handy. And, as he did so often at times when a man could feel lonely, he thought of Bea, fair and full-figured. He had never seen her equal, not even in saloon art. Sometimes he found it hard to picture her face, and yet he knew he would recognize her in a crowd at a half mile. How in blazes could she have gone off with that squirt West Pointer? Thel often punished himself by wondering what fault he had that had turned Bea away. It never occurred to him that Bea, being an ambitious as well as adventurous young woman, had simply done what she thought best.

Next morning there was a rime of frost on Thel's bed tarp when he awakened. The sky was still gray and only the twinkling of the last and brightest stars assured him that it wasn't about to rain. Ossie was already up and had fastened nose bags of grain on the saddle horses. The smoking campfire was slow to get hot. Thel put on his pants and shirt before leaving the covers. Then he sat on his bed and pulled on cold-stiffened boots.

"Your bear might be hard to skin this mornin'," said Ossie, clumping by with a bucket in either hand.

Thel grunted his agreement. This was the hardest frost of the season. But it gave a tang to the air and sweetness to the water. Thel Riley was happiest in the fall.

He was adding wood to the fire when Ossie called him. "Thel!" The older man's voice had a quaver in it.

Riley looked in the direction of the creek where Ossie had gone for water. He saw him backing away from the willows, then tripping and half falling in his haste.

There was some splashing in the creek and the whiplash sound of willow branches cracking. Before Riley could recover the rifle lying beside his bed, four horsemen burst from the screen of willows.

Indians! They rode into the camp, obliging Ossie to backtrack before them. Thel raised his hand in welcome and forced a smile to his lips. The Indians raised their hands too. But they did not bother with the hypocrisy of a smile.

CHAPTER FIVE

Two of the men were mixed bloods, swarthy-skinned and wearing scraggly mustaches and goatees. The other two were full-blooded Shoshones with thick black hair parted on the right and falling to their shoulders.

"How!"

"How! How!" The Indians trotted their ponies around the camp. When the Marstons, clad only in long, cream-colored underwear, scrambled from their blankets, the Indians reined in.

Henry Marston had picked up his 1886 Winchester and was standing on his bedding at a kind of parade rest. Imposing as he may have been in coat and tie on the floor of the New England stock exchange, in his long underwear H. B. Marston was ludicrous.

The Indians spotted the bagging seat in Mr. Marston's underwear and his rounded belly just visible under the woolens. They began to laugh. One of the full bloods slipped from his pony and, to the delight of his companions, did a brief duck walk. He added to this by hiking his blanket and wiggling his buttocks. He accompanied this with rooster crowing and other, less elegant barnyard noises.

Realizing that he was being mocked, H. B. Marston hastily donned trousers and shirt. "What is it they want, Riley?" he asked.

"They're Shoshones. Chief Washakie keeps his people in line, mostly. But I never saw an Indian that didn't want a present. Ossie, see if these fellows will have breakfast with us."

The Indians would indeed have breakfast. While Ossie fried antelope steaks, pancakes and eggs, the Indians sat with Thel and the Marstons.

The two mixed bloods wore worsted vests and soiled gingham shirts above their leggings. On their heads were flat-crowned gray hats with bright red bands. The other Indians, in ragged homemade shirts and wearing Hudson's Bay blankets around their hips, were bareheaded.

One of the latter, a man of about thirty with a bad burn scar on his right cheek, was the spokesman. He told the hunters that the Shoshones had been true friends to the whites. He said Washakie was the greatest of all the chiefs. Their chief had killed and eaten raw the heart of a Crow warrior. The site of this grisly meal was now called Crow Heart.

Had the Great Father in Washington ever done such a thing? the Shoshone asked.

"No," said Thel, he had not. But the Great Father knew of such things. He had given his great friend Washakie a shining medal and had a fine house built for him. He had given many presents to his children the Shoshones. He was strong, so strong that he did not have to kill his enemies.

The Indians looked at one another. Disbelief was written on their faces but they didn't argue. Instead Scar asked, "Why do you come to kill our game? We do not come to your homelands and kill your game. Why do white men play at killing our game? The buffalo are gone. The elk do not come to the river meadows any more. They stay high in the mountains where they are hard to find. Even the antelope are no longer plenty. Why do you kill our food?"

Thel said, "The Shoshones have always given us meat. We do not forget that. Now, if you will come with me, I have a bear to skin. There is more fat meat than we can use. We would like our friends the Shoshones to take this meat."

The Indians discussed this offer among themselves. One of the breeds was inclined to rob the hunters, seizing what they wanted, rather than take a handout. He was overruled.

While they gave no sign of it, both Thel and Ossie Adams understood what the Shoshones were saying. And they exchanged glances of relief when the Indians decided not to try robbing them.

"Ossie," Thel directed, "get that big round of cheese. Maybe these fellows would like some."

Ossie did as asked. But when he produced a large round of Cheddar the Indians were unimpressed.

"No," said the spokesman emphatically. "Pluggem up Shoshone."

After breakfast the Indians wiped their greasy hands on their leggings and stood up. Thel had decided to take Eugene Marston with him and leave his father in camp as a backup for Ossie. He could not be sure there were not more unfriendly Indians in the group.

Before Thel and Eugene left, Henry Marston called his son. "Here is some money. Buy us that sheep dog."

As Riley was already too well aware, Eugene was a moody young man. This morning his mood was sullen. "Oh, Father, what would we do with a cur like that? It probably isn't even housebroken."

H.B. smiled. "I expect you're right. The dog's probably never been inside a house. But he has the heart of a lion. When you find that and brains too, buy it. Now, please do as I ask." Marston pressed some cash into Eugene's hand then stepped back and waved the pair on.

As the two hunters left camp the Indians swung their horses in beside them. Eugene was briefly concerned that men he regarded as savages took such liberties. Then, as the ride proceeded without incident, Eugene began to enjoy and become interested in his new companions.

The Shoshones were completely uninhibited. They blew their noses with their fingers, belched loudly, and made other noises seldom heard in polite Boston society. What is more, the Indians laughed loudly about this. They patted their stomachs and swayed from side to side in their saddles to emphasize the noises they made.

Eugene began to laugh. In response, the Shoshones' antics increased and became even more outrageous.

"Boys will be boys," said Riley as one of the Indians stood in his stirrups, bent forward and wiggled his backside.

Next, without thinking or asking Thel's advice, Eugene pulled a pint of gin from his coat pocket. He took a drink, then passed the bottle to the Indian riding beside him. The Indian immediately clapped the bottle to his lips and began gulping the liquor.

"You've started something now," said Thel, frowning.

Seeing the bottle, the other Indians immediately encircled the drinker and set up a clamor. Reluctantly the Indian lowered the bottle and it was immediately snatched away by one of the grasping hands.

Eugene smiled happily as the Indian tipped the bottle to his lips. The others immediately began yelling at him and grabbed at the bottle. When one did succed in wresting the pint, the gin was nearly gone. In two more gulps it was gone and the Indian hurled the empty bottle against a rock. He howled with glee when the glass shattered.

The pair who had swallowed the most gin were already reeling in their saddles. One of them rode up beside Eugene and heatedly demanded more liquor.

"You're gonna be lucky if they don't pull you out of your saddle and strip you, lookin' for more." Thel Riley was angry and a little worried too.

He said to the Indian who had not had anything to drink, "Hold on, there isn't any more. You keep your boys in line. We don't want any trouble."

The Indians' suddenly ugly mood frightened Eugene. He had read lurid stories about booze-crazed redskins. He had not believed them until now. The feeling of euphoria that his eye-opener had produced disappeared. He rode closer to Riley, "I'm sorry. I had no idea a couple of drinks would cause this."

Riley regarded Eugene coldly. "You might have got us into a pile of trouble. Two of 'em are pretty drunk. Let's see if they can still ride."

Riley slapped his horse across the withers with his reins. The big sorrel responded, breaking into a gallop that excited Eugene's horse. It also plunged into a run. It began so quickly that the unprepared dude was nearly thrown backward out of his saddle. Somehow Eugene's hand caught the saddle horn and he was able to keep his seat. In so doing, however, he dropped one of his reins. The horse knew this immediately and veered off the route Thel was taking.

"Whoa! Whoa!" With one hand Eugene was clutching the saddle horn and dragging back on the lone rein with the other. He was swaying dangerously in the saddle, off balance and out of rhythm with his horse. Just before he was about to tumble, a brown hand shot from nowhere and seized his horse's bridle. Eugene dropped his remaining rein and clutched the saddle horn with both hands. The Shoshone pulled his horse to a stop.

The young hunter was so thoroughtly frightened that he could barely grip the saddle horn. The Indian slipped quickly from his own saddle and pressed the dangling reins back into Eugene's shaking palms.

As he did so Riley galloped up. "What happened?" he asked.

"This damned horse ran away with me," Eugene panted.

Thel looked at the Indian who was standing beside the head of Eugene's mount. The Indian shrugged, saying Eugene had dropped one of his reins. The horse had not understood what to do.

"That sounds more like it," said Riley. "Old Jim there is used to bein' ridden with both reins."

Eugene nearly made an angry reply, then, thinking better of it, said nothing. To the Indian who had stopped his horse he smiled and handed over a silver dollar. The man grinned and displayed the shining coin to his companions.

"Dammit, Eugene. They're all gonna' expect a dollar now. Ask me before you give these fellows presents." No sooner had Riley spoken than the other three Indians, all intoxicated, crowded their ponies around young Marston.

Fortunately he had a dollar for each of them. But he was much subdued and trotted his horse to Riley's side. "I'm sorry, Thel. I never realized how differently these fellows think."

Riley smiled and lifted his horse into an easy trot. "Never mind. It was my fault for runnin' the horses. A good trot will keep their minds on ridin', not stripping us."

The near runaway and now Riley's spine-jarring pace subdued the Indians' high spirits. The remainder of their ride to the sheep camp was uneventful.

Viro Pocket was absent, apparently moving the band of sheep. Accordingly the hunters passed through the camp and rode directly to the bear's carcass. After dismounting and tying their horses, the men crowded around the bear.

The Indians were obviously impressed. They regarded Eugene with awe until Thel explained that it was Henry Marston who had killed the bear. Then two of them helped Riley roll the bear onto its back so the skinning could begin. Eugene seated himself on a large rock to watch.

The two tipsy Indians crawled under a tall sagebrush and fell asleep. The other two squatted beside the bear and mostly watched.

"These boys want the claws and teeth from your bear more than they want the meat," Riley told Eugene.

"I imagine those are the parts Father wants most, too, in addition to the skin." Eugene was repelled by the appearance of the skinned carcass. It strongly resembled a naked muscular man.

"Is the grizzly bear much like this one?" asked Eugene.

"In a way. This is a very big black," said Thel. "It's as big as a smaller griz. And havin' Pocket's bullet in his shoulder made him damn mean. Course, when a grizzly gets on the fight there's nothin' worse. I think we were

lucky to blood you on this one. Now you'll know what to
expect if we get too close to another bear."

The smell coming from the bear, combined with its
human appearance and Riley's comments, made Eugene
shudder. Nevertheless Eugene found himself enjoying and
becoming interested in certain parts of this trip.

But he could not understand why his father considered
hunting the main route to manhood. Eugene thought, *Look
at those two drunken Indians asleep over there. They've
probably hunted all their lives.* Eugene saw no evidence
that it had done them any good.

Eugene had heard the popular theory that killing off the
wild game would force the Indian tribes to become farmers.
Farming, it was argued, had a civilizing effect. The Indians
had only to understand that taking up farms would improve
their lives. While Eugene pondered that and his lack of a
bottle, Viro Pocket appeared.

"Tarnation!" Pocket exclaimed. "That there bear is even
bigger'n I made him out. Where did I hit him?"

Thel pointed to a small, bloodshot wound on the bear's
thick shoulder. "Your aim was true," said Riley, "but your
gun ain't big enough for bear. The ball only went far enough
to make the bear mean."

Viro's weathered features assumed a scowl. He said,
"I've shot many a deer and antelope with this here rifle."
He patted the weapon's battered stock, further marred by
Viro's initials burned into it. "This is ol' 'meat-in-the-pot'
for me."

Thel nodded. He was thinking of all the animals Viro
must have shot and wounded with his peashooter. Some of
the old hunters claimed there weren't nearly as many
coyotes until the wagon trains began appearing. Every
pilgrim, it seemed, had a gun and the urge to use the game
for target practice. Thousands of animals were crippled and
lost to the coyotes every year. It made the Indians mad as
hell.

"Viro," said Eugene, approaching the sheepherder, "my
father wants to buy your dog, Tige."

"Tige ain't for sale. You seen for yourself what a spunky

bugger he is." The sheepherder reached down and roughly scratched the head of the nondescript dog standing beside him.

"I'll give you ten dollars for him," said Eugene.

"No, sir. There ain't money enough in your poke to get this here dog away from me. Why, I've seen him stand off a lobo wolf that was comin' in on the sheep."

Eugene smiled. "Will you take fifteen dollars?"

Pocket stamped his foot. "I told you, you ain't got the money it'd take to buy my dog. I raised him from a pup. His ma was the best herd dog I ever seen."

"I didn't realize Tige meant so much to you," said Eugene, entering into the spirt of the bargaining. "I'm authorized to pay you fifty dollars for him."

Thel Riley stopped skinning to stare at Eugene in disbelief. Fifty dollars!

He saw a tightening around Viro's eyes and the herder pulled his whiskery mouth half shut. "No, sir. Tige means more'n that to me." A nervous tic began jumping in the corner of Viro's right eye.

"What does he mean to you?" asked Eugene.

Viro took a deep breath. "One hundred dollars."

"Seventy-five is the best I can do," said Marston.

"Sold!" Viro exclaimed as he stuck out his hand, palm up.

Thel shook his head and went back to skinning. He would be lucky to clear that much for a week's outfitting.

Eugene counted some large bills and then several coins into Pocket's hand. Then he watched as the sheepherder fastened a long rope around the dog's neck.

"You better keep this rope on him for a time. Otherwise he might try to find me." Viro fitted the money into a buckskin roll and stuffed it deep into his layered clothing. Then he clambered onto the back of his long-legged horse and rode off.

Tige was a lop-eared pooch with one blue and one brown eye. His shaggy pelt was spotted with patches of gray and black interspersed with snippets of tan and white hair.

Looks were not one of his attributes. The dog sat quietly at the end of his rope and watched Viro leave.

The Indians had been more interested in watching the transaction. But they seemed to forget it when Thel resumed skinning the bear.

The work went swiftly until the end of each leg was reached. Then the guide had to proceed carefully on the paws, trimming each toe so that the claws remained with the pelt. Once that was done, he severed the bear's skinned head from the carcass. Finally Thel removed a chunk of back strap and rolled it inside the hide.

The packhorse brought along to carry the trophy balked. It was a lanky bay whose eyes bulged until a ring of white showed all around them when Thel approached with the bundled hide.

"Whoa, now!" Thel gripped the animal's lead rope to discourage him from rearing. It did no good. The animal reared and struck at Thel with his forefeet.

Acting quickly, one of the Indians leaped at the horse and seized the halter. Then, while holding the halter and pulling down on it with one hand, he gripped the bay's ear and twisted it with the other hand.

"That's it," said Thel, moving hand over hand down the lead rope until he stood beside the Indian. The Indian then tightened his grip on the bay's ear. The more the horse fought, the harder the twist on his ear, until he stood quiet but trembling and sweating. Thel placed the wrapped bear hide between the forks of the packsaddle and tightened the cinches. Next, with a few quick ties he roped the disputed parcel securely to the packsaddle.

"He can roll now and it won't come off." Thel took the lead rope, looped it around the saddle horn on his own mount and swung aboard. "Best we get movin'," he said. "Travelin' will give this packhorse something else to think about besides buckin'."

As the hunters left, the Indians were hacking at the bear, cutting off big chunks of dark red meat. Eugene reined in behind the packhorse. And Tige, trotting beside the young man, followed obediently at the end of his lead rope.

The warm Indian summer days of yellow grass and sage shimmering on the distant hills were ending. Now the sky was padded with thick gray clouds that spread eastward before a driving wind. On the western horizon a storm was building, one of those rain- and hail-lashed attacks on retreating summer. The temperature would drop and snow could fall on the high peaks. Riley eyed the threatening sky. He wanted to reach Fort Washakie before the storm overtook his party.

Viro Pocket was also watching the weather. A bad storm could scatter his sheep. He would have to move them into a protected valley and herd them closely. Otherwise his scattered animals would be easy prey for lurking coyotes and wolves.

He wished he had kept Tige until the storm passed. The dog wasn't as good as he'd told the dude, but he was a top sheep dog nevertheless.

The four Indians made quick work of the bear's carcass. The heavy layers of meat had been cut away from the shoulders and rump, then slung across their horses' backs. Just enough room was left for the men to sit their saddles. While they had appeared to forget Eugene's purchase of the dog, actually they had taken it all in. As they rode, the men exclaimed to one another about the thick wad of "dog" money Viro had tucked under his coat.

Eugene gave it no more thought. His father had given him one hundred dollars to buy the dog and he had done it for seventy-five. Looking at the animal he led, Eugene supposed a better-looking dog could be found on any Boston street corner. Still, there was something different about this creature. Tige remained calm but alert. He watched the men and horses carefully. There was no sign of homesickness.

When Eugene looked down at the dog, Tige looked back and wagged his tail. But he seemed to be his own dog—not a hand-licking tail wagger willing to fawn and beg for food or a pat. And Eugene would not soon forget how Tige had attacked the bear.

"Damn," thought Eugene, "I wish those Indians hadn't

swilled all of my gin." He felt the painful tightening in his belly. The screwworm of anxiety in his brain told him that his body needed alcohol.

The threatening skies infected Thel with their gloominess. He loved September, but a day like this was also a reminder of the swirling snows and bitter cold that were sure to come in just a few weeks.

He also thought about knocking Eugene's rifle aside as the bear charged. Had it really been necessary? Could he have been mistaken? Eugene had never said a word about it. And he did not seem the type to shoot his father in the back. The kid drank too much. But when Thel was a kid he had also drunk too much. He'd had a reputation on the Sweetwater for getting roaring drunk on payday nights. At the time he had assumed it was natural behavior because everyone did it.

Later, when he was older, he realized that everyone did not get drunk on payday. Everyone did not puke and have a pounding head on Sunday morning. Still, a drink after a long, cold ride warmed and relaxed a man. Thel Riley tried to keep an open mind.

The building storm recaptured his attention. They were running late. He hoped to reach Fort Washakie by the next afternoon. A heavy rain, however, would turn the road to gumbo. That sticky muck accumulates on the horses' hooves and turns the wagon wheels into slime-covered doughnuts.

If a storm made the road impassable his dudes would be marooned in a chilled and dripping camp. Dudes tended to dislike such accommodations. It made them snappish and critical. Thel jerked the rope on the packhorse and clucked his own horse into an easy trot.

Eugene accepted the faster pace. There was a bottle, one of several, hidden in his duffel. He yearned for it. "Come on," Eugene tugged the rope around Tige's neck. The dog obediently broke into a trot and kept abreast of his new master.

At the sheep camp Viro Pocket watched the heavy, dark clouds bearing down on him. An excitable man, he began yelling at his dog, giving commands no dog could understand let alone obey.

"Damn you!" Viro yelled. He wanted the bank of sheep driven under the lee of a big ridge a mile distant. The dog understood that Viro wanted him to run at the sheep and bark. But he could not understand where Viro wanted the sheep taken. From where he stood in the sage the dog could not even see the big ridge.

Impulsively dismissing the dog, Viro began flailing at his horse. He sent it lunging heavily through the sage and alarming the sheep, who lacked the collective brains to know what anyone wanted them to do.

As a result of Viro's panic it took twice as long to move the sheep as it should have. When the flock finally reached their destination they were upset. Viro and his dog had to head them several times before the sheep settled down and began to nibble. The first few drops of rain were falling when Viro put up his little tent in the lee of the big ridge.

Meanwhile the Indians were riding toward Fort Washakie. They also anticipated a storm, but it did not excite them; they had been caught out many times before. They would find cover, build a fire and eat bear meat until the rain stopped. One said they should have taken that rich white man's new dog. The dog was young and probably tastier than their old bear. They all laughed at the thought of eating such expensive meat. None of them had ever seen a dog held more valuable than a couple of ponies.

The four travelers found a sheltered niche in one of the ridges out of the rising wind. They dismounted and made a fire. When the rain began they were eating bear meat with their knives and fingers. Finished, they pulled their blankets higher around their shoulders, oblivious to the water streaming down around them.

Riley and Eugene overtook the wagon before the storm struck. Henry Marston waved happily to them as the riders came abreast of the wagon.

"Hello!" called Mr. Marston. "I see you got my dog. Splendid! Well done, Eugene."

He then asked Riley, "Could we make Fort Washakie before the storm hits?"

"We'll do our best. Ossie, kick their tails a little. We're gonna' get wet."

Ossie grumped and scowled. But he slapped the team's rumps with the reins and the animals leaned into their collars.

The rain was preceded by a chilling wind. The men buttoned their coats and turned up the collars. Eugene's silly go-to-hell hat was ripped from his head. Riley loped after and retrieved it. "You're gonna' need this," he said, handing Eugene the hat.

No sooner had Eugene replaced his hat and pulled it down over his eyes than the rain struck. For a while it pattered down gently and then the skies opened. Lightning flashed and crackled angrily along the ridge tops. The thunder boomed like ten thousand cannons, frightening the horses and making them want to run.

The men struggled into their slickers. Rivulets of water were streaming from their noses and off the toes of their boots. When the road began to soften and clutch at the wagon wheels, Thel and Eugene tied onto the wagon with lariats. Dallying the ends of their ropes around their saddle horns, the men used their mounts to help force the lumbering wagon through the muck.

It had grown very dark. The dense clouds advancing from the west blotted out the sun. Viro Pocket had circled his flock for the third time, talking to them and using the dog to turn strays back into the flock. When the lightning flashed and was followed by a terrific thunderclap, the nervous animals jumped to their feet. The blatting and baa-ing added to the herd's mounting hysteria.

"Now friends, now friends," Viro pleaded as he sloshed through the mud. Around and around the flock he went, keeping the animals turned, not letting them mass for a stampede. Eventually the shock waves of thunder and lightning passed over. These were replaced by a steady downpour. The sodden sheep became quiet and began lying down. Viro circled the herd a final time, then headed for his little tent.

The soaked canvas loomed like a gray ghost in the murk and rain. Viro's dog growled. "Hell's fire, dog," he said. "It's only the tent."

Viro strode forward, muttering. Suddenly a form rose in front of him. "What?" Viro's words died in his throat. He was struck from behind by someone swinging a club like a baseball bat.

The force of the blow drove Viro forward into the mud on his hands and knees. Blood poured from his nose and ears. He scarcely felt it when furious hands struck repeatedly at him with knives. Viro Pocket sank face down into the muck. His silent attackers stabbed his corpse again and again. Finally one waved the others back and rolled Viro onto his back. A hand ripped at the buttons on Viro's ragged coat. The hand slipped inside the coat, searching and slithering like a hungry snake. Eventually it emerged, clutching the leather case containing Viro's money.

The dog money. He had had it less than a day and it cost him his life.

CHAPTER SIX

IN THE DARKNESS THE ROAD WITH ITS WATER-FILLED RUTS
was only a gray blur. The draft horses strained in their
collars and occasionally slipped to their knees.

"Come on, boys!" Ossie urged the team forward. Blobs
of mud flew from their hooves, spattering Ossie and the
wagon. Thel's big horse bowed his neck against the wagon's
pull and fought his way ahead. Riley glanced at Eugene.
The young man, his hat pulled low and slicker glistening
wetly, stayed at his task. His horse also worked powerfully
against the wagon's pull.

Henry Marston was delighted. He enjoyed seeing men
and animals work hard under difficult conditions. He was
proud of Eugene's efforts. "Hie on, boys. You're doing it.
Just a bit farther. We'll make it!"

Thel felt he was doing his best without Marston's
urgings. Then it occurred to him that these were among the
first compliments he had heard from his client. Henry

Marston was a man who routinely expected more from men and beasts than he had a right to.

Through the slanting rain Thel glimpsed the low buildings of Fort Washakie. Beyond them stood the tepees of the Shoshones, smoke hanging heavily around their tops.

"Hallelujah!" called Riley. "You'll sleep in dry beds tonight."

As the drenched men and horses splashed into the Army compound they were challenged by a sentry.

"Thel Riley with the Marston party. Will you tell the duty sergeant we're here?"

The sentry disappeared into the rain. It had been previously arranged for the Marstons each to have separate quarters on Officers' Row. A Captain Speer was in command, and in addition to Riley's request, Speer had received orders from Army headquarters to see to the Marstons' comfort. Riley and Ossie were assigned a room in the livery barn.

When the sentry returned he was accompanied by a second lieutenant in a well-cut cloak. "Welcome to Fort Washakie, Mr. Marston," said the lieutenant, saluting, then shaking hands. "The captain sends his compliments and hopes you will dine with him this evening."

Thel looked on with disbelief. The Army he knew was usually correct but seldom friendly. Henry B. Marston must be some punkins indeed, to command such attention.

Spurning the lieutenant's offer to help him, Marston climbed stiffly down from the wagon. "Thank you. We are pleased to be here. Do you suppose we could have a hot bath?"

"Yes, sir. Sir, the orderlies will have hot water for you immediately. There are tubs in both your rooms. If you will show us your baggage I'll have it sent to your rooms."

"Thank you. Come, Eugene." Marston fell in beside the lieutenant and was shown to his room.

As the two Marstons splashed away through the rain, Thel and Ossie looked at each other. Rain was dripping from Thel's hat brim and streaming from his shoulders. Ossie, still seated on the wagon, resembled a wet airedale.

"Guess they ain't gonna draw a 'bawth' for the likes of us." Thel grinned.

"No. And we ain't eatin' with the cap'n, neither," said Ossie.

"Wouldn't have it any other way," said Thel, turning his horse toward the livery barn.

Ossie said, "Today I've had bath enough to last me till Christmas. But I wouldn't mind tryin' some of that millionaire's grub." Ossie clucked to the team and the willing animals once again leaned into their collars. They would soon be nuzzling into sweet prairie hay and rolled oats in the livery barn.

A private assigned to the stables helped the two men unhitch and feed the horses. The soaking harness, saddles and wagon tarps were hung up to dry. A fire was built in the small stove in the hostlers' room. Thel put on a coffeepot and the two men changed into warm, dry clothes. Thel fried steak and potatoes while Ossie sorted out the damp gear. After dinner the men wiped down and oiled all the guns.

When he had finished cleaning Eugene's lever-action Winchester, Thel threw it to his shoulder. The rifle pointed naturally and the action was as smooth as butter. Thel said, "I'm orderin' one of these after the hunt." Then he looked at the weapon and recalled seeing Eugene pointing it toward the back of his father's head. Carefully, thoughtfully, Riley slipped the Winchester back into its scabbard.

In earlier years Thel would have drifted over to the sutler's, bought a couple of drinks and a box of cigars. But tonight his back ached and he felt sleepy. He was propped up on his bunk smoking a last cigarette when a figure appeared in the doorway.

Thel glanced up and a grin spread across his creased face. "Tyghee! Howdy, my friend!" Thel jumped up and waved the visitor into the room.

"How, how!" Tyghee raised a brown hand, then extended it to fast-pump the hands of Riley and Ossie. If a white man had shaken his hand with such a light grip Thel instinctively would have distrusted him. But Indians often shook hands that way.

Tyghee was dressed in buckskin pants and a new peppermint-striped shirt with a purple neckerchief fastened at the throat by a big silver concho. Over his shirt he wore a black vest with beading on the pockets. Perched squarely on his head was a new gray Stetson with the crown sharply peaked, trooper style.

Tyghee was a full-blooded Shoshone and a relative of the great chief Washakie, "The Rattler." He had helped guide several illustrious dude parties into the Yellowstone country, the most illustrious being President Chester A. Arthur's grand cavalcade in the summer of 1883.

While Riley considered himself a competent outdoorsman, he acknowledged Tyghee as the best hunter he had ever known. The man's ability to track game was legendary. Ossie said, "Tyghee can track a chipmunk's shadow."

While the three old comrades became reacquainted in the barn, Henry Marston and his son were dining on snowy linen with the fort's commander. Captain Speer was a veteran of the Indian Wars and many years in the Army of the Platte. A widower, he had coveted this post in the warm valley of the Wind River. The Shoshones were "good Injuns" and their powerful chief, Washakie, kept them that way.

At other posts it was the Army's task to run down young bucks who jumped the reservation to steal horses and raise hell. Here, Washakie was master. His young men did not steal horses or harass the white settlers. But if they came home with a Cheyenne pony or if an Arapaho was found scalped with his throat slashed, Washakie appeared not to notice.

The Great Father in Washington had a house built for Washakie. It was fitting, the Government decided, that a great chief live in a house like a white man, not in a tepee like a blanket Indian. Washakie, however, stabled his favorite pony in the house and continued to live in his tepee. A visit to this chief in his camp was accepted etiquette for all important visitors.

Over coffee Captain Speer said, "You will find the old

boy most amusing. He loves having his photograph taken. And he will expect you to bring a present when you visit him. I suggest either a pony or a bottle of whiskey."

The elder Marston, elegant in a frock coat and dazzling white linen, said, "What if I give him one of each?"

"He will take you into his tribe and give you a feathered bonnet," said Speer. "He might even try to sell you one of his daughters."

Mr. Marston, his newly tanned skin gleaming in the lamplight, smiled. "Ah, Captain," he said, "with ladies as lovely as these for company," Marston smiled at the two women he'd dined with, "a squaw would never tempt me." He asked his son, "Eugene, do you think there's a Pocahontas for you in some tepee?"

Eugene had drained his wine goblet several times. He was leaning back in his chair, one arm hooked over the back. "Not likely, Dad, not likely." Eugene was drunk.

The two ladies smiled, then glanced at each other for reassurance that the smiles had been proper. Vivian Speer was Captain Speer's only daughter. She attended a school for young ladies in the East and had brought one of her teachers out West with her for a visit.

Vivian Speer was proud to serve as her father's hostess. She knew that Henry Marston was rich and the owner of much valuable real estate including a handsome country place on the Jersey shore. She also knew that Eugene Marston was a drunkard. But he was a *rich* drunkard. Vivian believed that the right woman could change the young man's intemperate ways.

Beatrice Woods, Vivian's teacher and companion, was not so sure. The widow of an Army officer, she had seen many a young man's career blighted by the bottle. One of her old beaus, a handsome cowboy called Thel Riley, had thrown some legendary benders in South Pass City when her father had a store there.

Bea gave her full attention to Henry Marston. He was the catch of this pair. Not that Bea hadn't had her chances after her young husband died of typhoid fever. From a lovely girl

Bea had become a handsome woman, shapely and with just enough silver in her honey-blond hair to make it gleam.

"Mrs. Woods," asked Marston, "I understand you are not a stranger to Wyoming?"

Bea still had her lovely flashing smile and she used it now. "No, my father had a business in South Pass City. We saw Indian raids, three-day blizzards, and desperadoes—everything Wyoming is noted for. There was a big store-room-dugout called 'the cave.' It had a heavy iron door. We took shelter in there a couple of times during Indian scares."

"Those must have been exciting times," said Marston.

"I'd rather remember them than have to live through them again," Bea replied.

"God, yes!" said Speer. "All I can remember of those days is being constantly in the saddle and always having the hostiles one jump ahead—or behind."

"I suppose you both have a point," said Marston. "But, really, living on the cutting edge and facing danger is the essence of life. It brings out the best in us. I think I have succeeded in business because I took risks—welcomed them, in fact."

Eugene waggled a finger at the captain's orderly, then pointed to his empty wineglass. The man hurried to refill it. All his father's talk about taking risks and accepting challenges annoyed him. He knew that his father bribed politicians and kept a firm of crooked lawyers on retainer to ensure that Marston and Company had no competition.

"It's *me* that's supposed to wrestle the grizzly and kill it with a knife," thought Eugene. He drained his glass, then noisily pushed back his chair.

"Ladies, Captain, I must go and prepare for the battle—in bed." Without another word Eugene pushed himself erect and walked somewhat unsteadily from the room.

Outside, the rain had stopped and it had turned cold. Partway to his quarters Eugene stopped and leaned against a convenient fence. His stomach rolled and his skin felt cold and clammy. He tried to heave but could not. Eugene straightened himself and walked, carefully erect, to his room. There he fell on the bed and went to sleep without undressing.

In the morning Thel, Ossie and Tyghee began inspecting the horses and mules the Indian had assembled. From here on, everything—from the folding sheet-iron stove to thread and sacking needles—traveled by packhorse. The team that had pulled the wagon from Rawlins was let out to pasture. Counting a few lightly loaded reserve animals, the party would start for the Yellowstone with twenty-two horses and mules.

"And not one of 'em's got shoes on," said Thel, shaking his head when the animals had been corralled.

"Did they ever?" asked Ossie.

Thel smiled. "No, and I never found a campsite with a stack of firewood split and a royal bull elk standing in the meadow."

Thel did most of the shoeing. Tyghee would not shoe horses. He helped by catching the animals for Thel and Ossie. The first day Thel shod a dozen head and could barely straighten his back that evening. Ossie shod two and was stepped on twice and kicked once.

"Damn it, Thel," Ossie complained, "I thought we got rid of the ornery buggers."

"The horses don't get ornery till you start whackin' 'em on the ribs with that rasp," replied Thel.

"Well, how else you gonna make 'em stand?" Ossie was indignant.

Thel shrugged. Ossie was not known for his patience. Thel Riley, on the other hand, was slow to anger. But when he became angry he was best avoided.

Next day the shoeing continued. Thel sent Ossie to oil harness and saddles while he and Tyghee worked with the horses. At midmorning he heard the *pop-pop* of rifle fire. The Marstons were practicing on the Army's target range. In Thel's opinion they would sharpen their aim better by working the sage for fleet Wyoming jackrabbits.

But no matter. The shoeing was nearly finished by noon.

The rain clouds had disappeared and the midday sun was hot. Thel's shirt was soaked with perspiration and his eyes smarted from dust and sweat.

His last horse was a long-necked bay with a blazed face running to pink on the nose. This horse, like most horses, had a fault. His was that while being shod he leaned on you. He did not kick or pull his feet away; he leaned.

No sooner had Thel picked up a hoof and positioned it between his knees than the bay began leaning. He transferred his weight slowly until the shoer found himself supporting one fourth of a horse. Although Thel tried every trick he knew to stop him, the bay continued to lean. As added insult, the horse relieved himself abundantly. Betweentimes he rolled his guts and generated some of the foulest wind Thel had ever smelled.

But when the bay nipped Thel on the rump, the guide exploded. "You knotheaded, son of a bitch!" Thel whacked the horse on the rump. "Stand up there or I'll knock the rest of it outta you!"

No sooner had he spoken than Thel looked up to see two people watching him. At first he ignored them, then he wiped his burning eye and looked again. *Oh, damn!* he thought. *It's Mr. Marston and a woman.*

Marston wore a bemused expression and a blush of embarrassment colored the tops of his ears. The woman suppressed a laugh. But as her eyes met Thel's she smiled broadly. "Hello, Thel. I never heard you say such things on the Sweetwater."

Thel's face went red under his tan. "My God. I mean, it is you, Bea, isn't it?"

"Surely fifteen years isn't too long to remember an old friend." Bea was enjoying Thel's embarrassment.

Henry Marston was not enjoying it. He had decided to pay some court to Beatrice Woods. He therefore resented her familiarity with his roughhewn guide, even if they were old acquaintances.

Marston said, "Beatrice, I've forgotten myself. These stables are no place for a lady. Please, I believe our lunch is ready."

Beatrice Woods took Henry Marston's arm and the two walked away. But as she was leaving, Bea turned her head and gave Thel one of her old heart-melting smiles.

Thel only took his eyes off Bea long enough to notice Tige. The dog was wearing a new, studded collar that was attached to the leash Marston was holding. Thel disliked what was happening to the dog. Ossie had orders to feed the dog a specially prepared meal every day at 5 P.M. Thel had liked the dog better when he was running free around the sheep camp and eating whatever Viro threw out. He wondered if the dog would still take on a bear if he became accustomed to all these luxuries.

Probably he was fretting about the dog because it took him a few minutes to accept meeting Bea again. When he returned to the troublesome bay he quickly nailed on the last shoe while ignoring the animal's annoying tactics.

He began to think about Bea. She appeared to have landed on her feet. He wondered what had happened to her husband, that slick shavetail. He'd find out—even if he didn't particularly want to know.

Tyghee had been sitting on the ground nearby. At first glance he appeared lost in some Indian reverie. Actually the man's dark eyes missed nothing. He could have reported the number and kinds of hawks and eagles soaring above the low hills. He knew there were antelope lying in the fold of a distant ridge. And he also knew that a small group of men were approaching the fort although it was still some miles away.

With the last nail driven and clinched Thel wiped his brow and threw himself down beside Tyghee. "Horses come," Tyghee said, nodding toward the south.

"Probably some of the soldier boys," said Thel.

Tyghee shook his head, no. "Not good," he said.

Riley had long ago learned not to question Tyghee in such matters. Thel had yet to see the approaching horses. He was looking southward with all the intensity he could muster. After several minutes of searching he saw a magpie fly up. Then the faintest trace of dust rose in the air. Finally Thel saw the riders, their forms misshapen and wavering in the heat waves.

There were six riders. As they approached, Thel saw that they were Indian police. A couple of them wore blue coats with big brass badges pinned on their chests. These men were part of a government scheme to have Indians supervise themselves. White rule, Washington reasoned, might not seem so oppressive if it were administered by red men.

One of the police was leading a piebald packhorse. Riley stood and walked toward the approaching riders. Even as he walked he saw what Tyghee had meant about "not good." A body was slung across the packsaddle and lashed to the cinch rings at the wrists and ankles. Of course the Indians would not have bothered to wrap a corpse in a tarp before bringing it in where there were women and kids. A corpse, to them, was just a corpse. And how could everyone see who it was if they wrapped it up?

Thel knew who it was. Even before someone grabbed the corpse by the hair and lifted up the face Thel knew. It was Viro Pocket.

Viro's clothing was blood-soaked. Captain Speer came out from his luncheon to examine the remains. "God!" said Speer, "the way they hack them up!" He asked one of the policemen, "Injun do this? You catch?"

The Indian shook his head. He was proud to have been in the group bringing in a white man's body. He stood by happily while the squaws and Indian children milled excitedly around the laden horse.

"Corporal," Captain Speer ordered, "take this body to the dispensary. I want the surgeon to examine it."

Thel came forward. "Captain, he was a sheepherder. Name of Viro Pocket. We killed a bear for him a few days back."

Captain Speer led Riley into his office and, with his adjutant taking notes, had Thel tell him what he knew of the late Mr. Pocket.

"Viro was a typical spooky sheepherder. Until I saw all

that blood I'd have guessed he went loco and rode his horse over a cliff. Looks like someone stabbed him."

Riley told the captain that Mr. Marston had bought Viro's dog. "His son, Eugene, paid seventy-five dollars for a *sheep dog!*"

Captain Speer was a responsible commander, but he had been in Indian country long enough to know that catching mysterious murderers was unlikely. Still, he immediately dispatched a detail to recover Viro's sheep and to investigate. Whoever owned the sheep would eventually come looking for them.

Speer then asked Thel, "Did you see anyone else in the area?"

"Lem Bischoff and three pals hoorawed my camp. But there were two Shoshones and two breeds at Viro's camp. They took the bear meat. And they were plenty interested when they saw Eugene Marston pay seventy-five dollars for a dog."

"Do you think they killed him?" Speer asked.

"Those bucks should have showed up here with that bear meat by now," said Thel. "You'll have an answer if they blow in somewhere with extra money to spend."

Riley also mentioned how Henry Marston had whipped one of Lem Bischoff's cronies back in Rawlins. Bischoff was known at the fort. He was a belligerent fellow, especially when he had been drinking. But the captain considered him more a troublemaker than a thief and murderer.

Riley pushed back his chair, preparing to leave. The captain held up his hand. "Just a minute. There is something else I want to discuss."

Riley settled back in his chair.

Speer asked, "How long have you been bringing hunting parties through here?"

"I started just after the buffalo finished—ten years. Why?"

Captain Speer picked up his pen and pointed it at Riley. "The Shoshones don't like it and I don't like it. This is their hunting grounds. You people scare off the game just as the Indians' fall hunts begin. They also resent it that most of the meat the sports kill is left to rot."

Riley had expected this. The captain was right. Game was harder to find than it had been ten years ago. But Thel blamed the white settlers and white, as well as Indian, market hunters.

"Captain, we follow the law—what there is of it. You know they're servin' elk and buffalo steak up there in Yellowstone Park. There's not an Indian in this camp that won't trade an elk hide for a rifle cartridge. If you've got five shells he'll kill five elk for you."

The captain's expression hardened. "That may be so. But the Indians have a treaty. You and your sports just rode in on the back of a wagon, so to speak. The game you kill is the straw that's breaking the camel's back. I won't have an Indian uprising on my hands just so you can live off the guiding business."

The guide resented the implication that his was an easy occupation. "Why don't you discuss this with Mr. Marston? He booked the hunt. You know he's big medicine back East."

"I discussed the problem with Mr. Marston. He doubted that the number of animals he and his son intend to kill would affect the Indians' meat supply. But I am telling you, Mister Riley: This is the last year the facilities of this post will be available to you and your hunting parties. Furthermore, beginning next season, my men will escort you out of this district if you come here to hunt."

Riley wanted to be angry. On principle he should tell this soldier boy off. Yet he knew Speer's complaints were justified. Thel was disgusted to see rows of dead deer, antelope, and elk hanging in front of town meat markets. He knew that day after day men filled wagons with ducks, geese, and sage grouse. A lot of the game spoiled before it reached the settlements.

"You could have a point," Riley replied. "But why pick on me? I run a clean outfit. You know yourself that some of your Army boys have come out and killed four or five times the game they could use. Clean up your own house before you start on mine."

Speer did not appear perturbed by Thel's response. He simply used it to put Riley on the defensive again, saying, "Follow your own advice, mister. That Marston boy has been drunk in quarters ever since you arrived. Now his father is talking about staying the week. But I want you off my post in twenty-four hours. I know Marston is influential but his son is a disgrace. Get him out of here."

Thel rose. "I'm sorry, Captain. I didn't know about that, bein' busy with my horses. But I won't stay here a minute longer than necessary."

Captain Speer saw from Thel's expression that his revelation about Eugene had been a complete surprise. He stood and offered Riley his hand. "That's one part of your job I don't envy." The two men shook hands and Riley turned and walked out into the company street.

Striding toward Officers' Row he went directly to the bungalow where Eugene Marston was quartered. Thel knocked on the door. There was no reply. He knocked again then tried the latch. The door was locked.

"Eugene, open up."

"Go away." Marston also cursed him.

Thel quickly located an orderly who unlocked Eugene's door. The shutters were closed and the room was dark. But in the gloom Eugene Marston could be seen lying half dressed on the bed. On the floor beside him were several bottles.

"What the hell do you mean, breaking in here?" Eugene propped himself on one elbow. He fixed a bleary eye on Thel, then reached for the Colt revolver lying on the bedside table. Thel moved quickly, kicking the table leg and sending the gun clattering into a corner.

Eugene then swung his fist at Thel. The guide caught Eugene's wrist, twisted it and threw the young man off the bed and onto the floor.

"Ow, damn you! Leave me alone." Eugene was whining.

Thel, still gripping Eugene's wrist, jerked him to his feet. "Come on, sonny. I want to show you something." Thel clapped Eugene's silly hat on his head and threw a coat over his shoulders. Then he pushed him out the door.

On the porch Thel said, "Now you can walk with me or be dragged."

Eugene's breath stank like a saloon slop barrel. He said, "Keep your damned paws off me, Riley. I'm coming."

Thel led the way across the compound to the dispensary. A white-coated orderly was sitting inside, reading a pulp novel. "We want to see Mr. Pocket," said Riley.

"Oh? I don't know about that."

"I do," said Riley. "Mr. Marston here had dealings with Pocket."

"Go ahead, then," said the orderly, returning to his book. "He's on the back porch—where it's cool."

As they passed through the small infirmary Eugene asked, "Who is Pocket? I don't know him."

"Sure you do. He's the sheepherder you bought the dog from."

"Oh? Well, I don't want to see him. Filthy fellow."

"You're not too sweet yourself." Riley pushed Eugene through the door and onto the back porch. In one corner there were two zinc-topped tables. On one lay the sheet-draped corpse of Viro Pocket.

"Take a look, Eugene. The captain and I figure you helped do this by givin' Viro too much money in public for the dog." Thel pulled the sheet from the body.

What he revealed shocked them both. Viro was stark naked. His skull was misshapen from the blow it had received and the face was black. The torso was torn and ripped by multiple stab wounds. The savagery of the attack was fully revealed and it was horrible.

When the enormity of what he saw registered on Eugene, he rushed for the back door. He began to vomit en route. Thel found him outside with the contents of his stomach partially on the ground and partially down his shirtfront.

As Eugene heaved he sobbed, "Oh God, Oh God."

Thel left him alone for ten minutes then said, "Come on, you got rid of everything. Thanks to you the captain has kicked us off the post."

They went to the stables where Ossie and Tyghee were put in charge of Eugene. "Take him for a long ride, Tyghee. The fresh air will do wonders. I've got to tell the boss that our welcome here has about run out."

CHAPTER SEVEN

Henry Marston was sitting with Bea Woods on the veranda of the commanding officer's residence. There was a bottle of wine in a cooler beside them and a stereopticon with boxes of views on the table.

"Ah, Riley," said Marston as the guide approached. "I've been wanting to see you. We'll stay here at the post a bit longer than you planned."

Thel glanced at Bea who gave him an amused nod. He said, "I'm sorry, sir. Did you know Eugene's problem had put him down? The captain feels we'll all be better off to get moving again. Him with that murder to handle."

Marston exploded. "I'm damned if some squaw-catcher junior officer can tell me—" He paused and glared at Riley. "Where is my son?"

"We thought the fresh air would be good for him. Tyghee is with him now. There's good fishin' in the creeks. I doubt they'll be back before supper."

Marston rose, then bowed slightly to Bea. "My dear, you'll have to excuse me. It appears that we shall be leaving sooner than I expected."

Bea nodded, smiling.

When the two men had walked out of her hearing, Marston's manner changed. He became ice-hard. "Eugene got drunk, didn't he?"

"Yes, sir."

"Damn it, damn him! I'm sure Captain Speer knows about it, too," said Marston.

"He knows. He's the one who figured we should leave." Riley hooked his thumbs in his belt. He got the feeling Marston wanted to blame him for Eugene's boozing. And that was something Thel Riley would never accept.

Riley also had mixed feelings about leaving. Since finding Bea again he had not had five minutes with her. Conversely, he resented seeing her getting so cosy with Marston. And wasn't he a smooth one with the ladies? Henry Marston forgot all about Eugene once he met Bea. Thel pondered the situation, then decided: Captain Speer was doing them all a favor. He and his crew would start packing at daybreak.

Ossie had been busy in the barn. Most of their gear and provisions was already packed in panniers or mantas ready for loading. The older man had prepared for so many pack trips that he wasted no time getting ready.

When Tyghee returned with Eugene, the young man looked better. His nose and ears were red from the sun. Tyghee displayed a fine mess of spotted trout.

Riley smiled. "That looks like supper. Eugene, your stuff is here. You might as well bunk with us tonight. We're leavin' early in the morning."

"And that way you can keep an eye on me." But Eugene's sarcasm was mostly show. He preferred the hunters' company to spending the last night at Fort Washakie being scolded by his father.

Thel's reply surprised him. "I'm your guide, not your

nurse. Do as you please. But you'd better be able to slap your butt in the saddle tomorrow mornin'."

As they talked Ossie and Tyghee were filleting the trout, then placing the orange meat in a hot skillet. They had fried potatoes mixed with onions, and chunks of crusty bread from the post bakery.

There was little conversation as the men ate their way through a huge meal. Thel was gratified to see Eugene eating heartily. The young man and Tyghee had already become friends.

Thel filled his mug with hot coffee, then lay back on his bunk to drink it. "Boys, this is huntin'. It's not just bein' out at daybreak trying to shoot something. It's also good food and good company, maybe that most of all."

He was interrupted by a tap at the door. Thel was startled to see Bea wrapped in a cloak and standing in the shadows. He went to her immediately. But before he could speak she took his hand and led him outside. The air was frosty but Thel didn't notice.

Bea said, "You didn't think I'd let you leave without a word, did you?"

"Your time seemed pretty well taken up by the boss. I decided we belonged to different tribes."

"Thel, you know better than that. Henry is a dear man. We know many of the same places. I've spent years in classrooms with silly girls. It's wonderful to be able to talk with someone like him."

"Sure it is. I do miss chatting with Commodore Vanderbilt."

"Don't be snide, Thel. It's not like you." Bea reached out and took Thel's big hands.

"Well, what do you want?" Thel sounded angrier than he really was.

"I wanted to see you, silly. I can't tell you how often I've thought of you over the years."

Thel replied, "I've thought about you. Always wondered what happened to you."

Bea was too wise to play the coquette with the big man

whose powerful hands now held hers. She explained that her husband had died of typhoid fever soon after they were posted to the Mexican border.

She said, "Harold loved me very much. Maybe more than I loved him. I couldn't refuse him."

Thel replied, "You refused me easy enough. When I told you how much I was makin' you said there was 'a big difference between living and existing.' I never felt so damned helpless. You knew I was doin' my best."

"I am sorry, Thel. Remember, I was very young." Bea raised her face and Thel kissed her full on the lips.

In the next minutes Thel was swept away. He hugged Bea to him and kissed her until she had to gasp for breath.

"Oh, Thel," she laughed, "let me catch my breath."

Bea made Thel feel more alive and happier than he had in years. He forgot how she had hurt him and how he had resigned himself to her marriage and never seeing her again. Now she had reappeared to rekindle old passions he had thought were long dead.

In the morning Thel sat up in his bunk and found Ossie watching him. "What's the matter?"

"Nothin'," said Ossie, who was cooking breakfast. "I just wanted to be sure we was still leaving this mornin'. You seemed to get powerfully busy last evening."

"We're leaving, don't worry." But inside, Thel was not so sure. He half hoped some problem would arise and force him to remain at the fort.

There are nearly always problems when five men, two dozen horses, and a dog set out on a ride of several hundred miles. Forgotten gear is remembered at the last minute. Pack animals are cranky and fight or lie down in the trail. Sometimes half of them disappear on the eve of departure. Packs turn and are bucked off; the horses must be repacked.

None of that happened on this morning. Despite the unspoken wishes of two men and one attractive woman, there were no delays. Thel saw Tyghee onto the trail at 8 A.M. with the Marstons and a dozen pack animals. There was no bucking and no tangling of lead ropes. It was as if Providence, or Fate, was helping the expedition.

Ossie left next with a five-horse string. Thel finished the packing alone. He would overtake the others around noon. His chosen mount was a big sorrel called Tom. Thel liked him for his stamina and fast walk. Thel had left Tom tied to a manger, and when he went to get him he found Bea there too.

"You weren't going to leave without saying good-bye, were you?" asked Bea. She appeared lovelier and more desirable this morning than she had last night in the moonlight.

"Sure I wanted to see you again. But I thought we said 'so long' last night." Thel put his arm around Bea's shoulders and looked down at her very tenderly.

"Don't you want to kiss me good-bye?" she asked.

"Sure, but I'm not shaved."

"I don't care, you big dummy. I want you to kiss me so it will last a long time."

Thel hugged Bea to him and kissed her while Tom munched contentedly at the hayrack. Only when the troopers on stable fatigue began banging brooms and buckets did Thel release Bea.

"Honey, I've got to go."

"I know," said Bea. "You have my address in Philadelphia. Promise you'll write."

"Sure. Maybe I'll even come to see you," he said.

Bea watched as Thel tightened his saddle cinches, then swung aboard. She had always admired the fluid grace with which Thel Riley mounted a horse. But she was not so sure how graceful he might seem to her friends in Philadelphia. Then, blinking back some tears, she waved good-bye to her man on horseback.

There were two ways to handle a pack string. The animals can be loose-trailed or tied and lead. By loose-trailing, a good packer can manage a dozen seasoned pack animals by driving them ahead of him. But when animals are green, or new to each other and the trail, it is more prudent to "tail up" and lead them.

Thel had tailed up, fastening the tail of one animal to the lead rope of the one behind. Although he had taken some green or potentially trouble-making animals, there were few delays.

He overtook the rest of his party while they were nooning in the meadow paralleling a creek. Some of the horses were grazing on hobbles. The rest were tied to nearby trees.

"Nooning" was mostly for the dudes' benefit. It was less work for the men to keep a pack train moving than it was to stop. Some laden horses were inclined to roll or wander. Tyghee and Ossie were keeping close watch on the stock.

Henry Marston was standing beside the small fire Tyghee had built to make tea. When Thel arrived Marston exclaimed, "By George, Riley, I am pleased that we left. Look at those mountains! Teeming with game, I have no doubt." Marston saluted the timber-clad peaks in the middle distance.

Thel was relieved to see him back on track again. "Yes, sir. Those mountains are the Wind Rivers. Tomorrow night you'll be campin' near the headwaters. Tyghee will show the two of you where to get a deer for camp meat between here and there."

Marston smiled and rubbed his hands. "Splendid. I've heard so much of Tyghee that I'm eager to see if it's all true."

"It's true," said Thel. "If it runs, hops, swims or crawls, Tyghee can track it."

Tyghee looked at Thel, a faint smile on his lips. He liked and respected Riley. He did not particularly like the white dudes he guided. But they paid him and that let Tyghee feed his large family while he went on hunting trips.

Some Shoshones did not hunt anymore. Instead they waited for government handouts. Tyghee thought this was bad. A man should hunt until he was too old to leave the fire. And then he should die.

Eugene, looking thoroughly miserable, said, "This trail

looks well used. I wonder that there's any game left around here."

Thel replied, "This is the main road the tribes use to Jackson's Hole. They're traveling, makin' their fall hunts now."

Ossie handed out steaming cups of tea. Henry Marston sipped his, then asked, "Are these Indians pacified? Could we have trouble?"

"The Shoshones have always been friendly," said Thel. "You met Washakie. He won't have it any other way."

"He didn't do much for that poor sheepherder," said Eugene. He was still recovering from his binge and seeing Viro's mutilated corpse.

"I never saw those two breeds before. They might have come down from Canada and talked the Shoshones into something," said Thel.

H. B. Marston interrupted, "So you think the Indians we gave meat to are the murderers?"

Thel threw the dregs of his tea onto the fire. "They were the only ones around that knew that Pocket had money." He did not tell the Marstons what Tyghee had said. From Thel's description Tyghee thought he knew the Shoshones. Bad actors, they had jumped the reservation before. They had stolen horses. Washakie had given them a final warning.

Thel clapped his hands. "Come on, boys. Ho for the Yellowstone! Think of all those poor buggers back in Boston scramblin' for pennies. You're gonna' have the trip of a lifetime!"

Marston grinned. "Splendid! I just hope we run into those murderers. Eugene and I will show 'em a thing or two. Right, Eugene?"

"Oh, indeed," Eugene's answer was studded with irony.

The grazing horses were caught and their hobbles removed. The pack strings were reformed and loads checked and retied if necessary. The work went quickly and the party was soon back on the trail.

This route generally followed streams that flowed through grassy, willow-dotted bottoms. It was easy to keep the outfit together in such terrain. But in the last big meadow before the canyon walls closed in and the grade increased, there was a problem.

The hunters overtook a large party of Indians preparing to camp. There were perhaps forty Shoshones—men, women and children. The women were erecting tepees. The Indian horses were loose and grazing while some of the children watched them. A few of the men were fishing in the stream while others sat by a fire and ate roast meat.

When Thel's outfit came upon them there was a tumult. The Indian ponies trotted up to inspect the newcomers. There was some tangling of lead ropes. The Marstons, who were in the lead with Tyghee, did not know what to do. They were immediately surrounded by Indian women who either begged or tried to sell them moccasins and beaded bags. The children scampered gaily through the pack string, some of them looking for items to steal.

This milling continued until Thel and Ossie arrived to end the confusion. No harm was done and the hunters were soon on their way again. Thel had given Bead, the headman, a packet of .45/70 cartridges. Henry Marston had purchased a pair of beaded moccasins for Bea at only twice the going price.

The dog, Tige, had handily whipped a snoopy Indian cur, then chased several others that had been snapping at the pack animals. Marston sent Tyghee to recover him.

When the Indian returned with the dog he tied a tight rope around its neck. He gave the rope to Eugene and returned to his regular duties a bit huffily, Thel noticed. One did not send a famous hunter like Tyghee to fetch a dog. Riley shook his head at the colossal ignorance of these rich Easterners.

The incident, however, was soon forgotten. They had reached their first camp, a meadow where the aspen and fir came down to the edge of the grass. It was a beautiful spot. There was a chance for deer among the aspens. And if the hunters were unlucky there were always abundant trout in the creeks.

They had stopped in midafternoon. While Thel and Ossie cared for the stock and pitched camp, Tyghee took the Marstons hunting. The horses were staked in the meadow with bells hung from the necks of three as a precaution.

The Marstons returned after dark. But even rank dudes knew from the tinkling horse bells and smell of wood smoke that they had found camp. Tyghee followed them in on foot. Loaded on his horse, its big antlers bristling from behind the saddle, was a fine buck deer.

Thel helped Tyghee hang the deer and unsaddle the horses. The weary Marstons stumbled into the firelight and sank down on the wooden panniers provided for them. Ossie handed them heaping plates of meat, potatoes, and fresh-baked sourdough biscuits. Thel heard them murmuring their appreciation. It always pleased and surprised dudes to get fresh-baked biscuits in rough camp.

"That's a fine buck," said Thel.

Tyghee nodded. He described how he had first smelled the buck, then found his tracks. He smiled when he told how the "old father" had doubted that he could smell deer.

Eugene was given the first shot but froze when he saw the buck. He levered cartridges through his rifle but did not pull the trigger. Finally Henry Marston took over and killed the buck in mid-leap with one shot.

"Boss, I hear you made a fine shot," Thel said as he and Tyghee walked into the firelight.

Marston, now much recovered from his exertions, beamed. "I wanted Eugene to draw first blood. That was the largest buck he'd ever seen. But he had a touch of buck fever. I'll admit I was lucky. But, damn, if that wasn't a fine shot. Broke the rascal's neck just as he was clearing a log."

While he never admitted it, Thel had begun to feel a certain remorse when a magnificent animal was killed. Sure, killing game was his livelihood and the happier his clients were, the more business he got next season. He thought perhaps he liked the animals more than some of the men who killed them, but whatever his reasons, he kept these feelings to himself.

Eugene was subdued this evening. He had suffered buck fever before. And he knew his father had enjoyed killing the deer. So maybe everything had turned out for the best.

Eugene had seen tracking and stalking he would never have believed possible. Tyghee had sniffed the air like a hound. Then he found the tracks and followed them at a fast walk. But as the spoor freshened, Tyghee became increasingly careful and intense.

Tyghee had found the buck in an aspen grove. Eugene could not see it. Among the sun-dappled aspens the golden leaves fluttered over a hundred shadows that might have been a deer. Finally Tyghee drew Eugene close to him and had him sight down his extended arm. There, at the tip of his index finger, stood the deer.

After his father had killed the deer Eugene felt sad and drained. The animal lay in the yellow grass at their feet. His big dark eyes were scarcely glazed as Tyghee ripped open the paunch and pulled out the guts. Eugene had reached inside his coat for a bottle. But it was not there. His lips tightened; he needed a drink.

In camp Ossie promised fried deer liver for breakfast. Henry Marston exclaimed, "Wonderful! Cook it with bacon. By George, this is superb. Pour me more tea, Ossie. Ah! Thanks very much!"

As Marston talked, Tyghee slipped up beside Thel and touched his arm. The Indian tipped his head away from the fire circle. He wanted to talk. Thel followed him down to the creek.

"What's up?" asked Thel.

Tyghee told him. When Marston had sent him after Tige in the Indian camp he had seen four men. Squatting in the brush and away from the others were two Shoshones he recognized, but the other two were mixed bloods he had never seen before. "I t'ink mebbe they at sheep camp," Tyghee concluded.

Thel pondered the unwelcome news for a few moments, then decided, "We better let sleeping dogs lie. We couldn't take 'em out of that camp even if we wanted to. We're bound to find some Army boys in the Yellowstone country. We'll report to them."

In addition Ossie was warned to be watchful, especially when he was alone in camp. Thel added, "Maybe havin' that dog in camp is a good idea after all."

Thel returned to his guests. The Marstons were basking sleepily in the fire's warmth. Thel offered to put more wood on the fire, but Henry Marston said he and Eugene were turning in.

He and Eugene were sharing a pyramidal tent called a miner's tent. Folding cots had been set up for them inside and their bedrolls placed on top. Thel Riley had long ago learned to keep his clients comfortable.

Because it was a clear night, Thel and his men decided to sleep in the open beside the campfire. As they crawled into their blankets some coyotes began to howl. They set up a fearful racket until some long and drawn-out howls silenced them.

Henry Marston called out, "Riley, did I hear wolves?"

"Yep." Riley's voice was dulled with sleep.

"Splendid!" called Marston. He ducked his head back into the tent and excitedly reported what he had heard to Eugene.

"Oh, hell, Father," said Eugene. "They'll keep. Go back to bed."

"Damn it, boy. Don't you ever get excited? Where's your enthusiasm? This is the life. This is real." Marston was wide awake.

"If you say so, Father." Eugene snuggled down in his blankets and tried not to think about a bottle.

When the camp was quiet again Ossie said, "I never knowed a wolf was 'splendid.' Do them fellers really believe they've growed up?"

"Go to sleep, Ossie." Thel worked his way deeper into his bedroll. He thought of Bea. Was she sitting in the Speers' parlor listening to Vivian Speer struggle through a piece on the spinet? Or was Bea telling some handsome officer about a play she'd seen back in Philadelphia?

Thel rolled over, made uncomfortable by his own thoughts. The moon had risen and he could make out the horses staked in the meadow. Occasionally one of the belled animals stirred and his bell clattered. Nothing seemed amiss. He could see Tige sleeping curled beside the Marstons' tent. He scolded himself for taking on troubles that didn't exist.

Then he looked at Tyghee's blankets. The Indian was propped on one arm and studying the horses in the meadow.

CHAPTER EIGHT

As MORNING'S FIRST GRAY LIGHT SPREAD SLOWLY OVER the meadow a horse's bell rattled. A doe and and two fawns jumped at the noise, then vanished into the mist that lay low over the creek.

It was time but Thel didn't want to get up. He was happiest in a place like this. The nighttime apprehensions had vanished with the darkness. He watched a raven drop from the limb of a snag, then swoop to a landing in the meadow. The bird marched around for a bit, then flew away, breaking the silence with its raucous cries.

Ossie was grumbling himself awake. Thel took pity on him and rose to rekindle the smoldering campfire. As he did so he saw that Tyghee's blankets were empty.

That was like Tyghee. He had slipped off into the predawn mists to scout around perhaps finding a fresh animal track or the footprint of some prowler.

Looking into the meadow again, Thel saw Tyghee

beginning to catch the horses. When he brought in the first bunch Thel asked Tyghee, "See anything down there?"

"Horse tracks," said Tyghee, pointing to the timber beyond the meadow.

"What do you think?" asked Thel.

Tyghee shrugged.

"Was it a stray?" asked Thel. Indian ponies often wandered in these meadows.

"Nope," said Tyghee. Then he turned and went after some more horses.

Thel's uneasiness came flooding back. The closing of the frontier had been like the tightening of a noose in this country. All the bad actors were being forced far from the settlements. They were drawn to remote areas like the Yellowstone and Jackson's Hole.

Once the party was on the trail again Thel told Henry Marston, "When Tyghee went to fetch your dog yesterday he saw four fellows off in the brush by themselves."

"What of it?"

"Tyghee thinks they're the four we gave the bear meat to. The ones at Pocket's sheep camp."

"Oh?" Marston sounded almost pleased. "Hadn't we ought to go back and take them in?"

Thel shook his head, "I doubt we could take 'em out of that camp without someone gettin' hurt. We'll likely see soldiers in Jackson's Hole or the Yellowstone. Let's let them handle it."

Marston started to protest, then reconsidered. "Perhaps you are right. But tell your men to keep a sharp watch. It would please me to help bring those fellows in. I'd like Eugene to have a hand in something like that. He should learn to confront dangerous men."

"Yes, sir." The guide moved Tom a few paces out in front. He did not want Marston to see his expression. Thel knew that any one of those suspected murderers could slit Eugene's throat and turn out his pockets before the young man realized what was happening. If Thel had to confront four killers he would not choose Eugene Marston to back him.

The morning's chill lasted until noon. Winter can come early in Wyoming's mountains. A foot of snow is possible any time after the first of September. The grass had already stopped growing. Accordingly Thel set a good pace. He did not want the Indians behind him to push ahead and take what was left of the good grazing.

Henry Marston was now riding with a holstered revolver on his hip. Most dudes liked to show off with a belt gun. But after a few days of having the heavy things tug at and batter their hips, most dudes put away their six-guns. Henry Marston was not entirely typical. Thel knew he could use the gun and would not be slow to do it, but Riley hoped they would not see the Indians again.

By the end of the third day the party was well into the Gros Ventre Mountains. The range was a hunter's paradise. There were many alpine meadows ringed with aspen and, higher up, thick stands of pine where game could hide. The party crossed the divide separating the tributaries of the Green and Snake rivers. Here they turned off the main trail.

It was among these high peaks that Riley expected to find bighorn sheep. The males of this species, the great rams with thick, curling horns, were often acclaimed the crown princes of western game. No animal had keener eyesight or lived in more difficult terrain than the bighorns.

The camp was made in the timber bordering a cluster of small lakes. There was good water and grass plus ample sign of big game. The fine weather held and put every one in good spirits. They agreed the first evening that Thel and Henry Marston would hunt the ridges south and west while Tyghee took Eugene in the opposite direction.

Thel said, "This is the place for those long-tom Winchesters. A big ram will keep his distance. You may have to take the long shot."

Next morning Thel sighted sheep within a mile of the camp. Using a battered brass telescope, he located a band lying under some distant rimrock. After careful inspection Thel declared that there were only two smallish rams with some ewes and lambs, but Marston had to see for himself.

Precious minutes were lost while the millionaire located the sheep with a pair of expensive German field glasses.

At midmorning Thel sighted more sheep. These animals were scattered along a steep hillside that was dotted with wind-twisted pines. This time a trophy ram was spotted standing half hidden behind a tree.

Marston bubbled, "Let's take him!"

From long experience Thel knew it was not that easy. He scooped up some dust from the ground and let it trickle through his fingers. He watched it drift to check the wind.

"He's already seen us and the wind is swirling. But let's try." Thel outlined a stalk and Marston eagerly agreed.

The horses were tied out of the ram's sight. Then, staying hidden in the draws and swales, they began climbing toward the ram.

The slope was steeper than it had looked from below. Moreover the ground was hard and covered with loose stones. Marston's feet slipped repeatedly.

"You got to be more quiet," Thel whispered. "He can hear those rocks rollin' down the hill."

"Sorry." Marston was puffing and red-faced. He was jealous of Thel's surefootedness. The guide never slipped or dislodged loose stones. And he did this in battered old boots with worn calks. Marston's boots had been custom made by the best bootmaker in Massachusetts. Marston was provoked to be the one slipping and sliding on the hill.

The higher they climbed the more Marston puffed. His aching thighs felt as if they were about to pop. In places the slope was so steep that even Thel half crawled across it. Marston did crawl, snatching brittle-looking shrubs for handholds.

In stalking the ram, the hunters twice came upon ewes and lambs. They had to lie low and let these animals move on, to spook them would surely scare off the ram. But the longer the stalk took, the less chance they had of finding the ram.

Finally the hunters gained the crest of the last ridge. They crouched there. When last seen, the ram had been 200 yards distant and slightly below where the men now hid.

Thel whispered, "I'm gonna' sneak up the ridge just far enough to see over. When I signal, you crawl up beside me."

Marston nodded. He welcomed the chance to rest and catch his breath.

Thel began inching his way up. He studied every feature of the emerging landscape. It was unlikely that the ram had stayed exactly where he had last been seen. Thel tried to avoid any careless movement that might alarm the animal. But when Thel was finally able to look over the ridge and into the next swale the ram was gone.

Calmly the guide uncased his telescope and lifted it into position. He systematically studied every foot of the dull-colored terrain before him. Nothing. He would look again.

The tiniest movement caught his eye. From behind a grayish boulder that was shaded by a scrub pine there appeared the broken tip of a ram's horn. The big sheep was lying down and almost hidden by the rock.

Thel carefully lowered himself out of the ram's sight. He saw Marston below him watching intently. He estimated that for Marston to have his shot they would have to crawl another forty yards up the ridge.

Motioning Marston to follow him, Thel began to crawl. He was heading for a low bush he judged to be at the point from which they could shoot. The ram was now more than two hundred yards off and slightly downhill. It was a tricky shot, but he thought Marston could make it.

Marston had began to climb. His labored movements suggested that he was both tired and tense. Thel expected that. Hunters got excited. The chase would not be worth the effort and expense if a man didn't get excited.

Thel returned to his surveillance of the ram. It was still lying down and showed no signs of being alarmed. Marston came nearer. Every time he moved, his boots dislodged a tiny shower of pebbles. Thel gritted his teeth.

When Marston was almost beside him Thel reached down and gripped the older man under the arm. Marston did not refuse the help. His face was deep red and he was panting like an old dog on the Fourth of July.

He could not see the ram. He located the boulder and the pine beside it but he could not discern the sheep. Thel smiled at the frustration stamped on Marston's face. The guide laid out his telescope, centered the ram in its lenses, then had Marston look.

"I see him!" Marston impulsively jerked himself higher and heaved the heavy rifle to his shoulder in the same motion. The ram sprang up and covered fifteen feet in his first bound.

The Winchester boomed and the heavy slug smacked loudly into the boulder that had sheltered the ram. Thel was on his knees and watching helplessly as the ram fled. He heard Marston reload and snap the breech closed, but it was too late for a second shot. The ram had vanished.

"I didn't think they moved so fast. I didn't even come close."

Thel said, "Your rifle shoots good but it also shoots slow. Once he started to run, your chances were next to nothin'."

Marston sat with his rifle resting across his knees. "Damn it, Riley, I let us down."

"No. That was a tough shot. You'll get another." Thel understood a hunter's feeling when he'd made a hard stalk, then missed his shot. He never mentioned that for the guide it was even more frustrating. The miss meant that the hard work of finding and then stalking a trophy animal had to be done all over again.

The men returned to their horses. Thel took some bread and hard sausage from his saddlebags. As he ate his dry lunch, Marston drank freely from the canteen. Between mouthfuls Thel scanned the surrounding heights with his telescope.

"All I see are a few scattered ewes and lambs. This afternoon we'll ride to that blue ridge yonder. Maybe your ram's on the other side." Thel stood and began bridling the horses and tightening the saddle cinches.

As they rode, occasional high clouds drifted across the blue sky. When a cloud obscured the sun, the combined chill of fall and high altitude was immediately noticeable. Marston's enthusiasm soon returned. He found the mountains exhilarating and enjoyed riding among the silent peaks. Thel led the way up the high ridge he had pointed out earlier. Marston followed close behind. His eyes searched the slopes and rims for game.

The ridge finally became too steep for easy riding. "Let's tie the horses here," said Thel. "I like to go on foot and stay off the skyline. We've taken some big rams out of this country."

Thel remembered the terrain. Below the ridge and on its far side was a rock-strewn valley with a small creek winding down it. Forage there was sparse, but at the top of the valley lay a fine basin. It had good forage and was a place favored by bighorn rams.

They climbed slowly and rested often. Marston was puffing and red-faced again. Thel didn't want him to suffer a seizure or mountain sickness. Besides, hunting was always better done at slow speed. The men saw no sheep but did glimpse several deer. Marston wanted to shoot a large buck.

"It's up to you," Thel had said. "But if you shoot a deer here you're not likely to see a sheep."

Marston agreed. The sheep was more important to him. He'd let Eugene and the Indian shoot a deer when camp meat was needed.

As the men climbed Thel suddenly stopped, listening. "Do you hear anything?"

"No. What was it?" asked Marston.

"Sounded like a bell," said Riley.

"No! Up here?" Marston was irate. They should be the only hunters in the area.

Riley didn't like it either but he climbed on. A man can hear lots of things in the mountains and never find their source. The Indians said they were the sounds of spirits. And they avoided certain places because they believed spirits lived there.

Sheep sign was scattered across the ridge. But Thel noted that none of it was fresh. There had not been a bighorn here in a week. Nevertheless the men climbed higher.

The wind increased and blew cold across the open slopes.

"Not much farther," said Thel. "We'll sit on the big outcrop ahead and have a look."

The outcropping was a great, shattered pile of gray-brown stone. After glancing around, Thel went to a spot overlooking the favored basin. "Damn it," he muttered.

There were no sheep in the basin. Someone had pitched a tent in the center of it. Staked all around it were four horses. Using his telescope, Thel saw the head of a huge ram lying beside the tent.

"Here," he said, passing the telescope to Marston. "Take a look at that sheep's head beside the tent."

"Thunderation! What a ram. Even at this distance he's huge!" Marston talked about nothing but the ram all the way back down the ridge and into camp.

He said, "I'm glad I missed that ram today. Why, now that we know the size ram it's possible to bag up here we should take our time and get one."

Ossie had been busy in the hunters' absence. He had dragged in logs to be used as seats around the campfire. A supply of wood was split and stacked beside the fire pit. Dutch ovens and grill were at hand beside a blackened crane from which were hung cooking pots. There were hot biscuits in one of the Dutch ovens and venison stew bubbling in a pot.

"Smells like supper is ready," said Thel as they rode into camp and dismounted.

Ossie stood by and took the reins of Marston's horse. "Ossie, I missed a fine ram today."

"Happens," said Ossie trying to sound sympathetic.

"A good thing, too," Marston continued. "We saw a magnificent ram later on. It's one like that I want."

Thel raised an eyebrow at Ossie. "That sure was a big ram. But it was already dead when we saw it."

Marston refused to consider that there might not be another ram as large in the entire range. "If there was one, there is likely another. Riley, let's visit that camp in the morning. I want a better look at that head. We might get some good advice from those hunters."

Thel said, "You're the boss," trying to sound agreeable.

Inwardly he was annoyed. Why couldn't Marston be satisfied with a good trophy? Hunters who wanted only the biggest heads often spoiled their own hunts. Furthermore Thel felt he did not need pointers from someone who intruded a spike camp into the midst of the area's best sheep range.

The mood was broken by the arrival of Tyghee and Eugene. Eugene said he had enjoyed the day, but he was snappish and uncommunicative. Tyghee said they had spotted a good ram at sundown. They planned to try for him in the morning.

When Thel described the spike camp in the basin Tyghee spat into the fire. "I think maybe Conroy," he said.

Thel Riley felt himself stiffen. Ralph Conroy was a braggart and a liar. He had been run out of Yellowstone country. His hunting parties left a trail of slaughter and waste behind them. There was no foul means Conroy would not use to get game for his clients.

He hunted at night with torches and carbide lamps. Conroy baited game with salt and then shot the animals over the licks. He used dogs to run game. He paid Indians to kill trophy animals for him, then he sold those trophies to his dudes who claimed them as their own. Conroy trapped bears over bait and had his hunters shoot them.

Some of Conroy's clients were ignorant. Conroy got the game for them and they assumed his methods were acceptable. Many an Eastern sport thought of Ralph Conroy as the Western mountain man who put on great hunting trips. Conroy had more customers than he could handle.

Henry Marston heard Tyghee mention Conroy. He said, "I've heard of that fellow. A bit rough around the edges, but colorful. I'd like to meet him."

"Conroy's not a friend of ours," said Thel.

"Come, come, Riley. Professional jealousy? This is the kind of small adventure that makes a trip. Let's meet him."

Eugene had not spoken. He had moments when he felt at the end of his rope. But there were big parts of this day that he had loved. Tyghee fascinated him. The man knew more about tracks and the creatures that made them than any of

the posturing naturalists he'd met. Tyghee was a savage.
His table manners were revolting. Yet the man was a model
of genuine kindness and concern. Once, in climbing a
ridge, Eugene had stumbled. He would have fallen if
Tyghee had not turned quickly and caught him. When he
was with Tyghee, Eugene felt like a little boy who holds his
father's hand on a walk through the park.

Eugene was glad they had seen the ram. Stalking it gave
him an excuse for not going with his father to meet Conroy.

"Eugene, wouldn't you like to meet the controversial Mr.
Conroy?" asked Marston.

"I'd rather do some hunting," said Eugene. "Tyghee
expects me to go out with him tomorrow."

"As you wish," said Marston. He wished that just *once*
Eugene would do what he wanted him to.

The hunters started early the next morning. Eugene
actually was cheerful as he and Tyghee departed. His father
was, as usual, enthusiastic.

"Splendid morning," he said, clumping around the fire
and drinking his tea.

Thel had a nodding acquaintance with Ralph Conroy. In a
Rawlins saloon Conroy had once pushed his way in beside
Thel at the bar. "You're Riley, ain't you? You know, I was
huntin' Jagg Creek an' Six Lakes before you even seen the
country. You newcomers should keep clear of us old-
timers." Conroy put a big smile on his mouth, but there was
no smile in his black eyes.

Thel replied, "There's plenty of room now. But every
outfitter ought to have his own district to hunt." Thel turned
to face Conroy. "But with everybody grabbin' all he can,
when he can, it'll be a while before that happens."

Conroy glared at Thel. "You tellin' me 'no'?"

Riley was just in from a long hunt. He wanted to relax
and enjoy himself. He said, "I doubt I could tell you
anything. And this is no time to talk business."

Conroy studied Riley like a dog deciding whether or not
to fight. Then he slammed his empty glass on the bar and
pushed himself away from Thel. As he went Conroy spoke

loudly of "wet-tailed pups" and how it was men like himself that had "made the country."

Heretofore Thel had been able to avoid Conroy. But now he and Henry Marston were entering the rock-strewn valley below the sheep basin. Thel said, "No tellin' where his main camp is. They could pull up spike camp in an hour. We might not see 'em."

It was wishful thinking. There was no logical way out of the basin other than back down through this valley. The pair had not ridden a mile before two riders with pack stock appeared on a rise ahead of them.

CHAPTER NINE

It was Conroy. A bit older and grayer of beard than Thel remembered him, but still the same bragging, blustering Conroy.

"Ah, gents," said Conroy, riding abreast, "if it's ram's horn you want, you're too slow." The guide gestured toward the packhorse he was leading.

Top-packed on the load were the horns and skull of a magnificent bighorn. The horns were huge at their bases and made a fine spread. Although the ram had battered away the tips of his horns they still formed a full curl.

"That's a forty-two-inch curl and two feet tip to tip," said Conroy's companion. He was a bearded man in his early forties wearing a fitted jacket of melton green with a matching cap.

Thel nodded to him. "Mighty fine ram. You had good luck."

The hunter smiled. "Thanks to Ralph. He packed in here last summer and salted the basin for me. When we came there were sheep everywhere. I took this fellow at seventy-five yards with one shot."

Marston spoke up, "I congratulate you, sir. We had a shot yesterday but missed. Now that I've seen your fine ram I'm glad we missed. By the way, I am Henry Marston; don't I know you?"

The hunter shook Marston's hand. "You should, Mr. Marston; perhaps the beard fooled you. I'm Earl Threadlow. I served as legal counsel to Amalgamated Transit when your company negotiated the Darrington contracts."

"Of course," said Marston who seemed to stiffen slightly.

Conroy broke in, "That's all big business. What we're talkin' here is big sheep. Riley, you won't get by showin' those lambs to Mr. Marston now he's seen a real ram."

Thel felt his cheeks burning. He knew Marston was going to give him a real grilling once the hunters separated. But before leaving, Threadlow invited Marston to bring Eugene and visit his main camp. It was located near the Gros Ventre River. He and Conroy were headed there now to hunt elk and bear.

"Thank you," said Marston.

"Come for dinner," said the lawyer. "I can promise you some prime mountain mutton."

As soon as they were alone, Marston started in on Thel. "Why haven't you salted some of these basins?"

"It's not sporting," said the guide.

"That may be true in the East," Marston replied. "But when hunters come out here at great expense and with limited time to take a full bag you should give them every opportunity."

"Mr. Marston, if you want to spend two months hunting sheep I'll show you a gigantic ram. But I won't salt and I won't jacklight, either. Remember, I told you my hunts are strictly fair chase." Thel was sincere. But inside he knew that some of his irritation with Marston was caused by his interest in Bea.

Marston raised his hand. "Don't misunderstand me. Threadlow is a crook. I don't imagine his hunting ethics are any better than his legal ethics. But he did get a superb ram. I'd like a shot at one myself."

"You'll get your shot," said Riley. He felt better knowing crooked clients booked crooked guides.

They did not get their shot that day. The hunting in the area had scattered and frightened the bighorns. Thel guessed, knowing Conroy, that there might be other rams lying dead and rotting on these ridges. Conroy was known to kill what he wanted, then leave all but the best heads.

After hunting all day the pair returned to camp. Ossie met them saying, "Tyghee and the young feller ain't back yet. I heard some shootin' way off yonder. Maybe they got something."

It was nearly 9 P.M. when Tyghee and Eugene came into the firelight. Tyghee was walking and leading his horse. Lying across the saddle was the grayish-brown carcass of a bighorn ram. Roped pack-fashion to Tyghee's back were the head and cape of a fine ram.

Forgetting his weariness, Marston sprang to his feet. "Eugene! Congratulations! You've outdone your father."

"Thanks to Tyghee, Father. He spotted the ram and then led the stalk. I just did what he told me."

"Good shot," said Tyghee, letting the ram's head slide from his shoulders.

Eugene Marston was as chipper and happy as Thel had ever seen him. "I would never kill another," said Eugene. "But being in these beautiful mountains and stalking sheep with Tyghee was a wonderful experience."

It had been a good day after all. Thel smoked a cigarette while Ossie removed and salted the ram's cape. Even Tige benefited. Ossie scraped flesh from the ram's cheeks and tossed it to the dog.

"How are you and Tige gettin' along, Os?" Thel asked.

"That is a smart dog. I didn't want him along, havin' to feed him special and all. But I guess he's about the best dog I ever seen. He don't bark 'less there's somethin' to bark at. Minds his business and keeps out from underfoot. And he ain't whinin' around and begging all the time."

Thel reached out and scratched the dog's ears. Why was

it, he wondered, that the Henry Marstons of this world always spotted good things first? Then they always had plenty of money to snap up the good buys. Thel thought ruefully of all the years he had tried to save up enough money for a place of his own. He was still a long way from having it.

But this mood quickly passed. Riley went to bed that night feeling good. Mr. Marston had not mentioned that Threadlow's ram was larger than Eugene's. Tyghee was satisfied with his hunters. Even the cranky Ossie had found a dog he liked. Sleep comes easily on such thoughts.

The camp awakened long before daylight. Thel had decided to relocate several miles to the west. He wanted fresh grass and territory that hadn't been hunted. He knew there were big rams in the peaks above Flat Creek. Marston and he would hunt in that direction while Ossie and Tyghee moved camp.

There was an alpine meadow where they could camp. From it they could move on to Jackson's Hole via either Flat Creek or the Gros Ventre River. Marston could have dinner with Threadlow or bypass him as he saw fit.

Henry Marston arose more enthusiastic than ever. The man was burning to bag a sheep larger than his son's, larger even than Threadlow's—if that was possible.

"By George," said Marston, "wouldn't I enjoy riding into Threadlow's camp and showing him a ram larger than his!"

Riley did not respond. He dreaded this kind of competition. It could sour a hunting trip.

But Thel need not have been concerned. They found few sheep of any kind that day. There were signs of Indian hunters, however. Riley guessed that a party of Sheep Eaters had preceded them.

"What sort of people are they?" asked Marston.

"About the sorriest kind you ever saw," said Thel. "They hunt with bows and arrows, sometimes try deadfalls. They live on next to nothing, if you can call it living."

"Wouldn't they be better off if the Army put them on a reservation?" asked Marston.

"It might stop their damned thieving. I've had 'em slip into camp at night and steal a slab of bacon or a pot. Tige is probably keepin' 'em honest on this hunt."

As the pair crossed a divide, four wolves leaped from beds in the brush below them. The hunters sprang from their saddles, jerking rifles from scabbards. Marston dropped two with his single-shot Winchester before the animals could reach cover.

Thel didn't fire. "Good shooting," he told Marston.

Marston was pleased. Killing the wolves took some of the edge off his obsession with killing a giant ram. Thel skinned the wolves, remarking that Marston had probably saved the lives of some sheep while collecting two handsome pelts for his den.

"I'd like to get some more. I'll have them made into a lap robe for Beatrice," said Marston.

Without replying, Thel hung the wet skins in a tree. Tyghee could retrieve them in the morning. Riley hoped they would not see any more wolves if it meant helping Marston get presents for Bea.

The sheep sign was sparse and Thel suggested they give up and find their new camp. Marston refused, insisting that they hunt until the last minute.

As a result they were late getting in. Thel had to fire signal shots for Ossie to hear and answer. It was nearly midnight before the pair sat down to supper.

Ossie said, "We thought you got somethin'."

"No, looked like Sheep Eaters hunted there a few days back." Thel took the coffee cup Ossie handed him.

Tyghee squatted across the fire from Thel. At the mention of Sheep Eaters he ran his index finger across his throat. He had helped soldiers hunt down small bands of Sheep Eaters in the Yellowstone.

Thel said, "Tomorrow we'll take a light camp and lay out a couple of nights. Mr. Marston wants to get his sheep and we should find one near the head of Flat Creek."

It was decided that Tyghee and Eugene would hunt elk around the main camp and also retrieve the wolf pelts. Thel and Marston would take a couple of packhorses and make a hunt to the west.

The mountainous country they rode through next day was wild and seldom traveled. Thel led, following a combination of Indian and game trails. They crossed breathtaking divides from which steep slopes and rocky cliffs dropped hundreds of feet into the canyon bottoms below.

"Riley," said Marston, "this is magnificent country. Surely there are mineral deposits here?"

"Lord, I hope not," said Thel. "I saw what the miners did to Montana. There wasn't a head of game left within miles of the camps. South Pass was about as bad."

"Progress has its price," said Marston. "The West needs workers, miners and farmers: lumbering, ranching. The sooner the wild Indians and the roaming white hunters are gone, the sooner the West can become a responsible part of the national economy."

"And the sooner I'll be out of business," said Thel.

"Don't worry. The process will take years. Good men such as yourself will find employment on the big ranches." Marston probably knew what he was talking about. But it was not a future, or fate, that Thel Riley particularly wanted.

While his hunting trip had been strenuous, Henry Marston had never before experienced hard, primitive hunting. Thel and his crew had done all the necessary chores. But when two men hunted alone in a wilderness the work had to be shared. For the first time in his life Henry Marston gathered firewood and helped with the horses. He laid out his own bed and peeled potatoes. And, like most dudes, he loved it.

Their camp was on the edge of a meadow dominated by tawny, sheer rock cliffs. "This is timberline," said Thel. "Wood is scarce and the feed is thin and won't last long. The plan is to get your sheep and leave as soon as we can." He never forgot the possibility of heavy snow even this early in the season.

But the glorious Wyoming weather held. By midafternoon the men were hunting in shirtsleeves. They found sheep, too—animals that behaved as if they had never seen a human being. They were easy to approach and did not run far if they ran at all. Only the trophy rams didn't cooperate. All the hunters found were young rams or older males with spindly horns.

Thel moved the camp again. Another day passed with no luck. They had seen some fine rams but none that approached the Threadlow trophy.

"We'll stay out a day or two longer," said Thel. "If we don't find a good ram here, we'll have to go north another sixty miles. You still have a lot of other huntin' to do."

Marston did not complain. Their fresh meat was gone and they were eating jerked venison and tinned beef with bacon. The onions and potatoes were gone. Thel baked bannock and served it with the last of the tinned jam.

"I didn't know bacon could be sliced so thin," said Marston.

Thel grinned at him. The real limit on their commissary was the forage. The men could always kill some kind of sheep, but the hardworking horses needed plenty of grass. Thel did not dare let the horses, who were mountain-trim already, grow thin and weaken.

So, on their fifth day out, it was with great excitement that Thel heard a remarkable sound. It was a whacking *crack* that echoed through the mountains like the smack of hammer on anvil.

"Hear that?" asked Thel. "That's your sheep."

The men were high on the side of a steep slope. It became too risky for riding so the horses were tied and left behind. They headed toward the sound by following sheep trails. Both men occasionally slipped, sending a shower of rocks bounding down into the depths below.

The cracking noise was repeated. Each time it grew louder. "We're gettin' closer," the guide whispered. "They're really buttin' heads. Be as quiet as you can."

Marston nodded. He was not puffing as he had on the first stalks for sheep. His tailored pants now bunched around his trimmed-down waist and there were hollows under his eyes.

The rams were facing each other on a wide ledge. Below

them was a short drop of twenty feet and then a steep slope that ended in a sheer drop one hundred feet above the canyon bottom. As the men watched, the rams charged each other. With lowered heads they collided head-on. There was a terrific crack of impact. Each was knocked back on his haunches by the fury of the attack. Thel had never known rams to begin cracking heads so early in the fall. But the guide seized the opportunity without questioning it.

The hunters had to crawl across a steep slope for fifty yards to get within range. Both men were panting with exertion and excitement when they stopped behind a low outcropping. The rams were 150 yards distant and so intent on battering each other that they had not noticed the hunters.

Marston carefully slid his rifle barrel out over the rock. Thel studied the sheep through his telescope. He had seen big rams before, rams as large as these, but never two such whoppers together. They both wore magnificent horns, broomed at the ends but massive and thick as a weight lifter's arm. They were not much larger than the Threadlow ram, but both were definitely larger. The only decision was which one to shoot.

Thel shifted his telescope from one ram to the other. He was mentally judging each, calculating the inches to the moment of decision.

The farther ram was larger of body, a great muscular fellow with many seasons in these mountains. The ridged surfaces of his horns likely bore the rings of a dozen years. His opponent was only slightly smaller, just as muscular but built nearer the ground. The tips of his brown horns were not as badly scuffed as those of his adversary.

This moment was Thel's. It was the traditional duty of the guide to judge the trophy accurately. He must tell his client without a doubt which ram was better.

Before Thel could speak, however, Marston's rifle boomed. The old ram with the worn horn tips made a half circle and fell on his side.

The surviving ram never hesitated. At Marston's shot he bounded forward, leaping from the ledge and landing on the steep slope beyond. Marston hit him in mid-leap. The heavy bullet broke the ram's neck and sent him sliding and rolling over and over down the steep slope.

Thel jumped to his feet, speechless. He saw Marston standing beside him with an expression of supreme delight on his face.

The second ram left a trail of cascading rocks and dust as he bounced and rolled downhill. There was a moment when the carcass appeared to pause on the edge of the drop-off. Then it rolled over the edge and crashed into the rocks at the bottom of the canyon.

It had never occurred to Riley that Marston would kill both magnificent animals. Either ram was the trophy of a lifetime. To kill them both was to diminish the supreme moment of a hunter's life. At least to Thel Riley it was.

But Marston was ecstatic. "Can you feature it. Two beauties! By George, Riley, you are the best guide after all. I am sorry to have ever doubted you. Pity the one went over the cliff. Do you suppose the horns are damaged?"

"Be a damned miracle if they're not." Thel gave Marston's outstretched hand a perfunctory shake, then started across to where the first ram lay.

Kneeling down beside the animal, Thel grasped the great horns and turned the head slightly. Even in death the ram was magnificent. The shock he felt at Marston's greed began to abate. He said, "You got the granddaddy of 'em all. This is a beauty. I never saw a finer one."

While Marston chattered excitedly, Thel began dressing the trophy. He handled the thick pelt carefully so as not to gouge or spot it with blood. As he worked he planned his course of action for removing the two rams from the rough terrain.

The second ram lay broken and bloody at the base of the cliff. This happened in sheep hunting. But Thel believed this was unnecessary. No creature as magnificent as this deserved to end smashed on the rocks. One of the great horns had survived the fall, but the other had been broken off several inches from the tip. Of course the meat was mostly pulp and shattered bone.

Working in his shirtsleeves, Thel stripped the bloody and torn hide from the sheep's skull. No taxidermist could recreate the ram from this mess. He found the broken piece of horn among the rocks.

Holding it against the remaining horn he said, "I guess this thing could be glued back together. It's chipped but it'll give an idea of what a fine ram this was."

Marston chose to ignore his guide's half-stifled anger over his killing of the second ram. He watched in silence as the guide skinned out the head then deftly separated it from the spine. He and Marston each carried a ram's head into camp on their backs that night.

The men were almost too tired to eat. But Thel insisted on opening their last tin of beef and heating slices over a fire. The men ate, then fell asleep in their blankets without undressing.

In the morning Marston found the strenuous labors of the past week had overtaken him. He was so stiff and sore he grunted each time he moved.

"You better stay here and make up the camp," said Thel. "I'll take one of the horses and get the meat. We should get started for main camp by noon."

They did not get started, however. In bringing in the remaining packhorse Marston dropped the lead rope. The horse immediately threw up his head and dashed off 100 yards. There he paused and, between nibbles of grass, looked coldly at Marston.

"Whoa, fellow, whoa!" Each time Marston approached him the horse trotted away. When Thel returned, the packhorse was still running loose. Marston was worn out from chasing him.

"Forget the bugger," said Thel. He put a packsaddle on Marston's riding horse and finished the packing. Finally he grained the horses and made sure the stray saw him do it.

The stray's appetite immediately overwhelmed his urge for freedom. He was soon crowding in among the other horses, nuzzling for grain.

Marston said, "I got him to come to grain. But he won't let you touch him."

Without replying, Thel took the lariat from his saddle. He went to within a few feet of the feeding horses, then stood waiting. When the stray raised his head to look around, Thel roped him.

"The less you chase a horse," said Thel, "the easier he is to catch."

The delay insured another night in the spike camp. Marston said, "Getting back to our main camp will be like checking into a first-class hotel."

The following day Tyghee met them a few miles above the main camp. He had become concerned and set out to find Thel. The main camp was in good order but empty save for Tige. The dog barked happily when he saw the hunters.

"Where's Ossie and Eugene?" Thel asked.

Tyghee shrugged. "Other camp." He explained that Eugene and Ossie had ridden to Conroy's camp the previous afternoon. They had not returned.

"We'll go after them," said Marston. "I want those fellows in that camp to see my sheep."

While Thel repacked both sheep heads on one horse he asked about the elk hunting. Bulls could be heard bugling all around.

Tyghee said, "Not hunt much. Stay in camp." The Indian had shot a spike bull elk for meat, but that was the sum of the week's hunting. Thel was annoyed. He had hoped to get at least one trophy elk here before moving north to the Buffalo Fork River.

They found Conroy's camp at one end of a big meadow bordering the Gros Ventre River. Grazing horses were scattered over the meadow. Smoke rose lazily from the stovepipe that jutted from one of the tents.

It must be a big party, Thel noted. They had many horses and several tents, large and small. He counted a half-dozen deer and elk carcasses hanging from the meat pole. Lying around the tents were antlered skulls of deer and elk. A black bear skin was stretched between two trees.

Thel hailed the camp. A man appeared at the front of one of the tents and waved them in. Riding closer, Thel recognized him as one of the men who had been riding with Lem Bischoff when they visited his camp.

The man grinned at Thel. "You huntin' strays?"

"Two," said Thel.

"I got 'em both. All our men is out huntin'. Your men couldn't make it."

At this moment Ossie appeared from inside one of the tents. Thel looked sharply at him. Judging from the number of empty bottles he saw lying around the tents, Thel anticipated a disaster.

Ossie was all right. "Glad you're back, boss. Howdy, Mr. Marston."

"Where is Eugene?" Marston's voice was very loud.

The camp jack snickered, "He's still on a party. Mr. Threadlow threw a whopper last night. Your man claims it ain't over yet."

"It's over," said Marston his voice cold.

They found Eugene sitting in a miner's tent. He had lost his boots and his silly hat was pushed far back on his head. There was a brown bottle between his legs.

"Hello, Father," Eugene spoke clearly but his eyes were red and watery. He had trouble focusing them.

"You scum," Marston reached out to grab his son. Eugene leaned backward to avoid his father. But in doing so he toppled over.

"Throw him on a horse." Marston whirled and stalked from the tent.

Eugene was too drunk to ride. So, with Ossie helping him, Thel loaded the young man across his saddle like a dead deer. He tied him there with thongs. "A mile of this," said Ossie, "an' he'll beg to ride astraddle."

Marston had already left. Thel and Ossie rode together, leading Eugene's horse and the packhorse behind them.

Ossie explained, "He hunted a little with Tyghee. Then he just quit. He fished a little and then he just wanted to sit around. He was meaner'n a wet bobcat. Then Conroy come by with his dude. Said they'd seen you up the country. Wanted young Marston to come to their camp. I figured I'd better tag along."

"You did the right thing," said Thel. "You didn't get drunk with them?"

"Aw, Thel, you know I'm tryin'." Ossie's tone reflected the pain he felt at Thel's question.

Ossie continued, "They was out to get him. That lawyer, Threadlow, knows Marston. It was a setup. Eugene made a fool of hisself. Gave Bischoff his boots."

"Bischoff?" Thel was surprised to hear that name again.

"Yeah, he's guidin' for Conroy. Besides Threadlow there's three other dudes in camp. All rich guys from back East. They don't care too much about huntin'. Just out to have a big time and raise hell."

Ossie described how the party had become a drunken orgy, Eugene had been abused. Bischoff and Conroy egged on the others. When he had protested, Ossie was knocked down and then shoved into a tent by himself.

Thel said, "Don't mention this. If the old man finds out ne's liable to shoot the bunch of 'em, Eugene first."

Shortly after this conversation Eugene began making unhappy noises. He was being simultaneously sick and begging to be untied.

Eugene managed to ride into camp on his own. His father was there ahead of him. He refused to look at his son. What Thel had anticipated as being a happy reunion became a cold, silent evening. Everyone turned in early.

Although the Marstons did not yet have their trophy elk, Thel felt it wise to leave this territory immediately. The farther they got from Threadlow and company the better. They began breaking camp at dawn. Thel gave Tyghee orders to avoid Conroy's camp as he and the Marstons left for Jackson's Hole.

Marston was still furious. He ignored Eugene and was barely civil to the other men.

Thel hoped a good long move to a new campsite would take everyone's mind off the Gros Ventre disaster. He planned to overnight somewhere in the northern end of the big valley that lay below the Teton mountains. They could hunt antelope and sage chickens on the flats overlooking the Snake River.

They could also fish. The river offered superb fishing. It was easy to land fifty trout in an afternoon's fishing. Some parties agreed to throw back every fish under three pounds. Others wagered on the heaviest trout or the largest number caught.

Thel would have preferred to hate Eugene's guts. He was a spoiled drunk who had notions about blowing off his old man's head. But Thel could not despise the young Marston; he was more inclined to pity him. Then he thought of Eugene's evil temper and sometimes irrational behavior. He would be glad when he finished this hunt. Riley turned his thoughts and efforts to packing horses and moving camp. For a few hours he wanted to forget the Marstons.

CHAPTER TEN

TYGHEE HAD FOUND A CAMPSITE AMONG A GROVE OF cottonwoods beside the Snake River. Thel was pleased when he saw it. There was good grazing, plenty of wood, plus excellent hunting and fishing nearby.

Tyghee was gone so Thel and Ossie set to work unpacking. They saw Henry Marston fishing at a bend of the river. Tige lay on the shore watching him. Thel guessed that Eugene was with Tyghee until he noticed the young man's horse tied in the grove.

As each horse was unloaded Ossie staked it among the trees. The grass there was knee-high. The leaves on the cottonwoods had turned color but had not yet begun to fall. In the distance the smooth surface of the river was a burnished blue. Across the river and looming up thousands of feet were the majestic Teton mountains.

If this place couldn't soothe the Marstons' troubled souls, no place could. Riley's mellow feelings were jolted by

Ossie's high-pitched yell. Grabbing his rifle, Thel ran to where Ossie waited.

The older man was kneeling in the tall grass when Thel ran up to him. Ossie was looking at something and Thel looked too. For an instant he scarcely believed what he saw.

It was Eugene Marston and he had been savagely beaten. He groaned when Thel helped him to sit up. The young man's face was a bloody smear: nose broken, his upper lip split and some teeth knocked out. Both of Eugene's eyes were purple and badly swollen. Thel thought Eugene might have been mauled by a bear.

"Help me," whispered Eugene, his tears streaking the dried blood on his cheeks.

The young man leaned on Thel and Ossie as they helped him back to the camp. They sat him down on a pannier, cleaned his wounds and treated them with an antiseptic. Eugene told them his father had beaten him.

"Your father did this?" Thel was remembering the beating he had received on the Sweetwater. Perhaps Thel had asked for that going-over. But he would never have believed a father, one who regarded himself as a gentleman, would do this to a son.

"I'm not the man my father thinks I should be. And I drink, you know." Eugene dabbed at his bleeding nose.

Thel looked at the nose, then placed a willow stick in each of Eugene's nostrils. Then he lifted them and set the broken nose. Eugene howled with pain.

Ossie could not help grinning. "I know. My honker got busted so many times I learnt to set it myself. When a man gets a few drinks in him he's liable to stick his snoot where it ain't supposed to be."

Eugene's nose was protected and held in place with an X of court plaster. Thel suggested that the young man go to bed. But he refused, preferring to sit by the fire while Ossie cooked supper.

When the camp was in order Thel shouldered his rifle and walked down to the river. Henry Marston was casting a pair of flies into the head of a swirling pool.

Marston let the current carry his flies into the heart of the pool and never raised his rod until he had a trout on each hook. Then he carefully played the fish, drew them into the shallow water and released them.

"Fishin' pretty good?" asked Riley.

Marston partially turned to reply but did not stop casting. "Very good indeed. But you really came to ask about Eugene, didn't you?"

"Yes." Thel was considering calling off the trip. He thought Eugene might want to see a doctor and certainly a dentist.

Marston said, "Eugene disgraced me. By drinking he spits on my good name and makes me vulnerable to my enemies. The embarrassing news of his latest debacle will reach the East before we do."

"You must have used that tricky Jap fightin' to beat him up so bad," said Thel. "At first I thought a bear had jumped him."

"Perhaps a bear could have taught him a better lesson." Marston reeled in two more flopping trout and released them.

Thel said, "I'm thinkin' of canceling this hunt. We can leave here and go over the pass to Idaho. The railroad's not too far. Maybe your boy should see a doctor."

"He doesn't need a doctor," said Marston. "And as for canceling this trip, you and I have a contract. The letter you wrote me set the conditions. I accepted them and made a cash deposit. Unless you want my lawyers to break you, don't even think of canceling this trip."

Although he was tempted to accept Marston's challenge, Thel decided not to, only saying, "Mr. Marston, I'm not afraid of you. But I don't want any more trouble. We'll camp here until Eugene feels better. There's a few white people in the valley now. If he needs one, I think we can find a woman to look after him."

"Rubbish. Eugene will be fine when I tell him to be fine," said Marston.

Thel walked back to camp. He wondered why men like Marston and Threadlow took hunting trips. They could spread more misery among more people back in the city.

They didn't need to come all the way to Jackson's Hole to do it.

Tyghee had returned to camp. The Indian had ridden up the Snake and forded the river below the big lake. He reported signs of other hunters in the area. Some were Indian and some white. The game was scarce and very shy. He had, however, found fresh moose tracks. Moose were uncommon in the area and it would be remarkable if they could bag a good one. Thel found himself chasing the theory that by showing the Marstons a fine trip, he could postpone their hacking each other to pieces.

Eugene was in no condition to go moose hunting. But when his father returned from fishing, he jumped at the chance.

"I told you," Thel reminded him, "bull moose are scarce. But if you find one, he won't be too tough to stalk."

Marston had shot a moose in Maine and was eager to bag one in Wyoming. He and Tyghee would set out the next morning at daybreak.

"I thought you were my guide, Riley?" asked Marston when Tyghee was mentioned.

"Tyghee knows where he found the moose tracks. He's hunted this valley since he was a kid. If there's a bull moose here, he's the one to find him for you."

Marston said nothing more. He and Tyghee left early the next morning. After the arduous sheep hunt, Riley welcomed the chance to put tack in order and catch up on chores.

At noon Ossie filleted and broiled some of the trout Marston had caught. Eugene emerged from his tent and joined them. No one mentioned that his father had caught the trout. Eugene said they were delicious.

While he washed the dishes Ossie said, "Thel, some of our spuds have froze and gone bad. We didn't have too many when we left Washakie. Do you think there's any farmers down the valley raisin' 'em?"

"Could be. What do you say, Eugene—want to see some more of Jackson's Hole? I'll leave first thing tomorrow."

Eugene agreed to go, provided he didn't have to show off his battered face.

"Don't worry," said Thel. "There's so many boys on the dodge comin' through here, almost everybody keeps his face hid."

Tyghee and Marston returned late that evening. They had found the moose tracks and followed them until it was too late to see. Marston said, "You're right about that buck Indian. If there had been a moon I believe he would have tracked all night. He's phenomenal. We'll try again first thing in the morning."

Riley was pleased that Marston liked hunting with Tyghee—even if he did refer to him as a "buck." Thel asked, "Do you want to take a light camp and stay out till you find him, like we did huntin' sheep?"

"I was about to suggest it," said Marston. Whatever his many faults might be, lack of enthusiasm wasn't one of them. The guides appreciated a hunter who didn't have to be coaxed out of bed in the morning.

The next day Thel and Eugene rode south to hunt potatoes while Tyghee and Marston went north after moose. It was one of the first overcast mornings since they left Washakie. Woolly gray clouds had settled on the Tetons' jagged peaks and cold wind blew from the southwest.

The valley trail bore the tracks of many cattle and horses. For several years a few cowpunchers had driven small herds into the valley and summered them there. Some then tried cutting the wild hay and wintering their stock in the valley. Thel did not envy the cowpokes who wintered in to feed the cattle. Jackson's Hole had long and bitterly cold winters.

The Indians never stayed there year-round. And it could be argued that the outlaws who used the valley as a winter hideout were not much better off than their colleagues in jail.

As they rode, Thel told Eugene about the outlaws including the prospector who had murdered his three partners on the Snake River the year before.

Eugene asked, "Is it dangerous to be riding here alone?"

He noticed that Thel was wearing his revolver for the first time since the trip began.

"It's not near as bad as New York after dark or even Larimer Street in Denver. Everybody stays watchful here. We're not likely to see a soul between here and the farms."

Thel's opinions were borne out at the first homestead they found. The only building was a small cabin near the river. A rickety-looking pole fence surrounded the cabin and a small garden. As the men approached, a skinny dog ran out barking.

"Hello!" called Thel. "Anybody home?"

The cabin door opened just wide enough to accommodate a long gun barrel, Civil War Springfield by the look of it.

"What do you want?" the voice was female and frightened.

Thel removed his hat. "We're hunters, ma'am. We thought you might sell us some potatoes. I see you got a milk cow. We'd buy your extra butter, too."

"We sold it to the store. You get away from here. I can shoot!"

"Oh, don't shoot, lady," called Thel. "We mean no harm and we're leavin'. Store down the valley?"

"Just follow the trail. Now get away."

Thel replaced his hat. "C'mon, Eugene. That woman is too scared to be safe." He swung his horse around, gave a tug on the packhorse's rope and loped out of rifle range.

The men located a second claim but no one was home and the place looked abandoned. Thel explained that some nesters only stayed in the valley during the warmer months. When fall came, they left. "Folks might come back next summer and find some stranger livin' in their shack. It's hardscrabble livin' here and sort of finders keepers, too."

Eugene grew silent. Out of the corner of his eye Thel saw his jaw working silently while he simultaneously tapped the saddle horn with his reins. Eugene's jitters were transmitted to his horse. The animal began to toss his head and prance sideways.

"What's the matter with this horse?" demanded Eugene.

"You. You're wiggling all over him. Keep it up and he'll throw you." Thel tried to smile.

"I could sure use a drink," said Eugene.

"Then stop right here," said Thel, dismounting and taking hold of Eugene's reins. "Get down," he said.

Eugene looked puzzled but did as he was told. He stood in front of Thel.

"Shut your eyes and open your mouth," said Thel.

"What for?" Eugene's confusion mounted.

"You said you wanted a drink," Thel's tone was commanding.

"This is crazy. I'm not a kid," said Eugene. Then he considered Thel's determined look and shut his eyes. Slowly his mouth began to open and a flicker of a smile tugged at the corners.

"Wider," Thel ordered. "And keep your eyes shut."

Eugene tilted his head back, eyes tightly shut. If his mouth had not been so tender he would have laughed. This was some kind of hick joke.

When Eugene's battered mouth was wide open and his eyes tightly closed, Thel drew his Colt and slid the muzzle deep into Eugene's gaping mouth.

He cocked the revolver and Eugene's blackened eyes popped open. Thel seized him by the shirtfront so he could not pull away.

"You want to kill yourself, Eugene. So just touch the trigger and take a drink of ol' Sam Colt. It'll save us all lots of misery. And it'll get the job done for you quick."

Eugene, his eyes bulging with fear, tried to pull away. But Thel jerked him forward and shoved the gun muzzle even farther into his mouth.

"I'm not going to find you a drink and I'm not going to pull this trigger. You'll have to pull it. You've got less control over booze than you have this gun. It's made a damn puking infant out of you. And you let it."

Thel stood there for a long moment, moving the revolver ever so slightly. And each tiny motion increased Eugene's terror.

Finally Thel slowly withdrew the gun barrel from

Eugene's mouth. "Remember this," said Thel, tapping the gun muzzle, "the next time you stick a bottle into your mouth. No one gives a damn if you kill yourself—except your dad. He cared enough to beat hell out of you."

Thel lowered the revolver's hammer, moved the cylinder onto an empty chamber, and holstered the weapon. Without a word Eugene Marston climbed back on his horse. Thel ignored him, swinging into his saddle and lifting the horse into a fast walk.

Riley felt cold sweat between his shoulder blades. He'd taken a terrible chance. What if Eugene had pulled the trigger? *Well, he's blowin' his brains out one way or the other,* Thel thought. *And he didn't pull the trigger.*

They rode until early afternoon. Eugene remained silent and Thel spoke only when it was necessary. Another homestead loomed out of the sagebrush.

"This one's got three shacks," said Thel. "I hope one of them's the store."

It was the store and also the occasional post office, bar, and meeting place for the scattered residents. John Gurney was the proprietor. The bulk of his meager living came from horses and cattle—both the ones he owned and those others stole and brought to him.

The store was actually just a corner in Gurney's one-room cabin. His shelves held a few basic supplies: flour, salt, matches, sugar, tobacco, and ammunition. There was a bench to sit on and, beside that, a keg of whiskey mounted on a sawbuck.

When his dog began barking, Gurney emerged from the cabin wiping his hands on a filthy shirt. "Howdy! It's Thel Riley, ain't it? Long time, Thel. Come in and have a drink with the boys." Gurney shook Thel's hand and patted Eugene's shoulder.

"What's the other fellow look like?" Gurney chuckled.

Eugene ignored him. And Thel looked away to take in the two saddle horses and a laden pack mule that were tied to Gurney's corral.

From the cabin's shaded interior a voice said, "Hey

Snub, the competition's showed up again." Lem Bischoff's burly figure rose up from the bench by the whiskey barrel.

Gurney asked, "You boys acquainted? Lem come in for supplies. He's huntin' with Conroy and some rich dudes up the Gros Ventre."

"Hello." Thel did not offer to shake hands. Eugene stopped stock-still in the cabin doorway.

The other man was the one they had seen in Conroy's camp when they went to get Eugene. His name was Snub Feeney. He was a small man wearing oversized and probably cast-off clothing. He appeared ill at ease when he recognized Eugene.

"Why, hello, darlin'," Bischoff leered at Eugene. "Did you fall off your pony?"

Eugene did not answer.

Thel spoke. "John, we was told you had spuds; maybe some fresh carrots and onions, too."

"Yes indeed," said Gurney. "Some of the first crops growed in this valley. Right fresh, too, and my price is fair."

Bischoff snorted. "Sure, ten bucks for a four-bit sack of taters is a bargain." He helped himself to another drink from the keg.

Thel said, "We've got a long ride. So maybe we'll just sack up the spuds and be on our way."

That seemed to relieve Gurney, who led the way to a root cellar behind his cabin. Lifting the heavy door, he revealed an earthy-smelling pit containing potatoes, moldy onions, carrots covered with soil, and several cabbages.

Thel brought in his canvas panniers and, with Gurney and Eugene helping, filled them with produce.

Gurney carried one of the laden bags to where Thel's horses were tied. Thel took the other. He set it down and carefully counted the currency and coins into Gurney's hand.

Bischoff was waiting for them in front of the cabin, one booted foot resting on a chopping block. "Didn't you tell ol' John what a robber he is? He didn't give sweetie-pie there a better price, did he?" Bischoff leered and winked at Eugene.

The young man reddened at the taunt. He swung around to face Bischoff, then exclaimed, "You're wearing my boots!"

"You gave 'em to me, remember. Or was you too drunk to know it? Cut quite a figure, didn't he, Snub?" Bischoff held one hand under his chin and waggled his fingers coquettishly at Eugene.

Instantly Eugene rushed Bischoff. His voice was high-pitched with emotion. "I want my boots!"

"Kiss off, pussy." Bischoff squared to meet Eugene and timed a clubbing right hand. The blow struck Eugene on the forehead, knocking him backward. But he did not fall and rushed Bischoff again.

This time Bischoff feinted clumsily with his left and hit Eugene flush on the cheekbone with his right. The young man dropped to one knee.

"Gene!" Thel called. "Leave it. Come on. You're in no shape for this." Judging from these preliminaries Bischoff was going to beat Eugene senseless. And Snub was standing just clear of the action with a single-shot rifle in the crook of his arm.

Bischoff did not advance on Eugene. He preferred to hold his ground and punch the young man when he charged. Eugene obliged him again, rising and rushing at Bischoff with fists flailing.

There was a smirk on the big man's face as he again measured Eugene. He swung a roundhouse right. But this time Bischoff missed. Eugene ducked and sidestepped the blow. Then, to everyone's surprise, he hit Bischoff squarely on the mouth. It was a lucky punch. And it made the man furious.

He lunged at Eugene, spitting blood. Eugene dodged away. Bischoff swung hard and missed again, throwing himself off balance. Seeing an advantage, Eugene rushed forward and tackled Bischoff around the knees. The pair crashed to the ground. Instantly the young man was on top of Bischoff, pummeling him with rights and lefts.

But Bischoff was far from finished. He grabbed Eugene's shirtfront. Ignoring the blows raining down on him, Bischoff forced Eugene to one side. Slowly the big man pulled Eugene off balance. He was too strong for Eugene. Twisting and then rolling, he threw Eugene off him and onto the ground.

Thel braced himself. He could not let Bischoff get on top of Eugene. But before Thel could move, Eugene's right knee shot up. He sank it into the big man's groin just as he was falling on him.

Lem Bischoff rolled up like a tumblebug, moaning and clutching himself. The fight was over. Eugene scrambled to his feet. Bischoff hardly moved as Eugene unlaced and recovered his boots.

The young man was panting. His already damaged face was beginning to swell again from Bischoff's blows. But he said, with obvious pride, "I got my boots back, didn't I?"

"You sure did," Thel replied. "He won't be ridin' any bucking horses for a while. But we'd better get out of here."

John Gurney said, "Thel, don't bring your friend back here again. He can't fight much but he sure is lucky. Bischoff will kill him the next time."

As they left, Thel looked back to see Snub helping his friend to a seat on the chopping block. "Guess that makes it two for the Marstons and zero for the Rawlins Rowdies," said Thel.

Ossie had a cheery fire burning when the men returned to camp. He laughed with delight when Thel told him how Eugene had won the fight and recovered his boots.

Ossie said, "You better smoke them boots good after Bischoff wore 'em. I'll bet he ain't washed his feet in six months."

Eugene sat by the fire and quietly ate his dinner. His manner was pleasant but he appeared lost in his own thoughts. When he had finished eating he dropped his plate and utensils into the wash bucket.

He said, "It's been quite a day. I'm turning in. Thank

you, Ossie. Thanks, Thel." He gave Thel a peculiar look, then disappeared into his tent.

The rain that had threatened all day arrived during the night. There was a violent display of thunder and lightning followed by sheets of cold rain.

In their tent Thel said to Ossie, "It'll be muddy in the mornin'. I hope Eugene decides to sleep in."

But Eugene was up at daylight, stirring the fire and making coffee. Thel appeared, stretching and rubbing his eyes. The sky had cleared and the temperature had fallen. The rain-soaked grass was coated with ice.

"You're up early," said Thel, warming himself by the fire. "What do you have in mind?"

"I want to climb that mountain." Eugene pointed to the tallest of the jagged Teton peaks rising above them.

Thel could not conceal his surprise at this request. He said, "I don't know if it's ever been climbed. Pretty rough country up there. It's covered with ice this morning."

"If you don't want to go it's all right. I'll go by myself," Eugene's battered face was a study in determination.

"I can't let you go up there alone," said Thel. "But hangin' by my fingers and toes ain't a part of this hunting trip."

"I've been studying the mountain with my field glasses," said Eugene. "If we leave by noon we should make the top and be back in a couple of days. I'll pay you one hundred dollars to help me reach the top of that mountain."

Thel accepted. But when Ossie heard the plan he was appalled. "What in hell did you give in for? You'll break your neck. We're huntin', not doin' kid stunts."

"I've got no choice, Os. And there's an extra hundred in it."

They had an outfit ready before noon: a blanket apiece, two ropes each fifty feet in length, and two small sacks of food. Ossie packed jerky, dried fruit, hard cheese, and tea with an empty tin can to boil it in.

Ossie also accompanied them to the base of the mountains. Before returning to camp with the horses he said, "If you're not back by day after tomorrow I'll send Tyghee to look for you. But think this over; it's a damn-fool stunt."

"I agree," said Thel "Now look after things and we'll be seein' you in a couple of days."

The guide had hunted in the Tetons, but he had never climbed very high. There was little game among the high, sterile peaks. The men spent the afternoon clambering up steep gorges filled with freshets and slippery rocks. They lost count of the times they had to backtrack. Sheer cliffs blocked one possible route after another.

Finally, however, they found a ridge they could climb. It led them toward the tall peak but ended in a basin far below the summit. There was a snowdrift ten feet high on the basin's shady side.

"Does this snow ever melt?" asked Eugene.

Thel saw dark lines running horizontally through the snow. He supposed they marked the winters. "It looks like this snow has been piling up here since Noah. You lookin' for an ark?"

Eugene smiled. "Not exactly. But maybe you're nearer right than you think."

They had stopped amidst some stunted evergreens, still below timberline. Thel broke dead boughs from the trees and tossed them on the ground. "At least there's enough wood. No one ever built a fire here before."

Thel made the fire in front of a huge boulder that shielded them from the wind. The blaze reflected heat from the rock. As long as the fire burned, the men were comfortable. They took turns getting up in the night to tend the fire.

CHAPTER ELEVEN

BOTH MEN SLEPT FITFULLY. BEFORE DAWN A BITTERLY cold wind began sweeping down from the peaks. It scattered the coals of their fire and sent smoke swirling over their beds.

"What a night," said Thel, sitting up. He was shivering and his bones ached from lying on the cold, rocky ground. On the eastern horizon he saw a pink-gold band of light. He hoped the sunrise would bring some warmth with it.

Eugene's youth buoyed his newfound enthusiasm for mountain climbing. But his head still throbbed and his body hurt from the blows he had taken.

He said, "It can't warm up too soon for me."

When it came, the warmth was not much different from the evening's chill. The men packed their belongings and climbed to the saddle above the basin. The exertion warmed them and they stopped to rest and enjoy the sunshine.

The silence surrounding them was nearly complete. Occasionally a pebble would fall from the ramparts above them. It clattered and cracked as it bounced from rock to rock. They watched as two gray birds with black-and-white trimming flew by.

"We must be pretty high," said Thel. "We're lookin' down on the birds."

Looming above them in cold, menacing silence was the great peak. As they trudged across the rocky saddle, each man studied the mountain. They agreed that the best route to the top was up the southwest face.

The first leg of the climb was relatively easy. The men left everything behind but their two lengths of rope. Each tied one end of his rope around his waist and slung the remaining coil over a shoulder. The mountain was becoming an enemy.

Thel led and was inching up a narrow ledge when he slipped. He had been climbing with his chest pressed close to the sheer rock wall. When he slipped, his hobnailed boots skidded sickeningly across the rock.

"Ice!" Riley squeezed his fingertips into a fissure in the wall and held on. Agonizing seconds passed before his hobnails bit into the rock. He began moving again and finally found a place where he was able to reach up and pull himself onto the ledge above. He crouched there, resting.

Then he looked down at Eugene on the ledge below. The young man seemed suspended in space. The abyss below him gaped wide, like a devouring mouth.

Thel lowered the end of his rope to Eugene. Using it for assistance, the younger man climbed the icy ledge like a monkey running up a pole.

As the pair knelt together on the ledge Thel said, "Don't look down. I did and it really made my guts suck up."

Eugene replied, "Heights never bothered me. Once, in New York, I went up on a tall building under construction. The foreman took me out on a girder where the men were riveting. The people on the streets below were just dots."

His mental picture of this made Thel's skin crawl. The higher he climbed, the more nervous he became. Moving crabwise up a sheet of slippery rock, he slipped again. This time he froze and slid three feet before his boots struck a jutting rock.

"Thel!" called Eugene. "Are you all right?"

"I wish I was someplace else."

"Rest a minute. I'm coming up." Eugene scaled the sloping wall easily. He loved climbing and was exhilarated by the danger.

Reaching Thel he said, "You rest here. I'll go ahead and throw you a rope." Riley didn't argue. With Eugene's help he readily scaled the slippery wall.

As the two men lay pressed against the side of the mountain Eugene said, "I'm getting the hang of this. Why don't you anchor me with the rope while I go ahead? Then I can anchor you while you come up."

Thel hesitated. Then he admitted to himself that the spoiled rich kid from Boston was a much better mountain climber than he was. The only sensible thing to do was to let Eugene lead.

As Thel grew increasingly tired, Eugene appeared to gain strength and enthusiasm. To Thel's dismay he began bounding from rock to ledge like a mountain goat.

"For God's sake, Eugene! Be careful!"

But in his concern for Eugene, Thel forgot his own anxieties. Almost unconsciously he began working *with* the mountain instead of fighting it. He used handholds instead of clutching at them, and braced his feet with confidence when he anchored Eugene.

This system worked and by late morning they were clinging to an outcropping just below the summit. Eugene planned to scramble up a chute above them. From the top of the chute he would step over to an adjacent ledge, then anchor Thel as he climbed. From the last ledge they estimated they could pull themselves onto the mountain's top.

Thel watched admiringly as Eugene climbed surely up the chute. He improved with each new climbing problem. Nevertheless Thel wedged himself tightly among the rocks and anchored Eugene. At the top of the chute Eugene breasted himself onto a tiny shelf, then stood erect. He was ready to make the long step across to the last ledge.

As Eugene stepped across a thousand feet of open space Thel braced himself, both hands gripping the rope. Eugene made it easily. As he turned to smile down at Thel there was the sickening crack of splintering stone. Part of the ledge had broken loose. Eugene threw himself forward, trying to reach the remaining bit of ledge. He almost made it. Then his feet slipped, his hands clawed frantically at the smooth stone, and he plunged off the ledge.

Thel thought they were both dead. When Eugene's body hit the end of the rope Thel nearly toppled. The line bit into his flesh like a meat ax. Somehow he held on. The rope burned through his hands.

Then Eugene was hanging upside down with his arms and legs flailing helplessly. As he skidded across the mountain's rough surface he resembled a runaway pendulum. Suddenly his hand gripped a rock. His body paused in mid-swing. Eugene righted himself and his other hand found a fissure. He hung for a moment, his feet dangling in space. But he soon found a foothold and then another.

Eugene rested spread-eagled against the cold Teton. Recovered, he called, "Climbing!" With Thel's help Eugene scrambled back to where Riley lay crouched against the mountain.

Forcing his cramped hands open, Thel looked at the friction burns on his palms. He placed the burning flesh against the cold stone. It helped.

"You earned that extra hundred just now," said Eugene. "Still game to make the top?"

For the first time and without understanding why, Thel wanted to reach the summit. He said, "We can't quit now. But be more careful. Fall off here and you're gonna look one hell of a lot worse than you do already."

Eugene smiled, then climbed back up the chute. At the top he took a new route to the ledge and reached it easily. He anchored Thel as he scrambled up beside him.

"We're nearly there," said Eugene. "Want to go up first?"

"Nope. Get a handhold. I'll give you a leg up."

There was no ceremony. Thel Riley boosted Eugene Marston to the top of the Tetons like one boy helping another over a fence.

For a moment there was no sound save the buffeting of the wind. Then Eugene called, "Come on, I've got you."

Gripping the rope, Thel climbed the final obstacle and crept out onto the top of the mountain. The area was larger than he'd expected. From a distance, mountaintops came to points. But when you were sitting on one it resembled the uneven surface of any other slab of rock.

Eugene was standing erect with the wind whipping at his clothes. Thel stood up beside him then sat down again. He preferred the relative security of the rock underfoot. Above, there was nothing to grab onto.

"It's even better than I thought it would be," said Eugene. He was surveying the sun-dappled panorama below.

"Those are the Wind River Mountains to the east," said Thel. "We're headin' up there." He pointed toward the snow-tipped Absarokas.

"You remember when you stuck your gun into my mouth?" asked Eugene.

"Sure." Thel regarded that with a different perspective today, on top of the mountain.

Eugene said, "I hated you for doing that. One reason I wanted to get you up here was to humiliate you. Do you think I *liked* that mess in Threadlow's camp? I know there's something wrong with me."

"There's something wrong with us all. I froze on that wall. And I don't like bein' up here near as much as you seem to." Thel eyed Eugene warily.

"A few minutes ago you saved my life," said Eugene. "But I was over wanting to get even with you last night. I feel rotten but I feel good, too. Does that make any sense?"

"Maybe. Until yesterday you never really did anything on your own. You beat Bischoff any way you could because you *had* to. You climbed this mountain. Maybe no one else in the world can say that. I know I can't. You were up here first and waiting for me."

Eugene sat down cross-legged and facing Thel. He reached into his coat pocket and produced a cigar. He carefully cut the cigar in two with his pocket knife and handed half to Thel. The wind made lighting the smokes difficult but they eventually succeeded.

"We're about two and a half miles high," said Thel. "I wonder if anyone ever smoked a cigar that high before?" The smoke made him giddy.

"Maybe we should leave the butts for the next ones up," said Eugene.

"Nope," said Thel. He lobbed his cigar far out into space. "The next fellow up here ought to find it just the way you did. We think we're the first. Let him have the same feeling."

"Agreed," said Eugene. He lay back and looked up at the sky. The cigar fell from his fingers. Thel watched as the wind sent it rolling across the rocks and over the edge.

When they felt rested the men began the descent. They used the same anchoring technique as they had in coming up. Eugene skittered over the rock ledges while Thel descended slowly and tried to avoid looking straight down. There were no more misadventures. They collected their possessions in the saddle at midafternoon and reached the foothills by dark.

They settled into a fly camp beside a spring and built a large fire. "Ossie will be watchin'," said Thel. "He should be waiting for us first thing in the morning."

The men finished the last of their provisions, saving only a bit of tea for morning. Marston said, "There's something else I want out of this."

"What's that?" Riley was drowsy but feeling good.

"For people to stop calling me 'Ewe-Gene'; I hate that damn name."

"Only one way to do it," said Thel. "Stop acting like him."

"I'm going to try."

As predicted, Ossie was waiting for them with the horses

when the two men walked out of the woods. "Did you climb it? We bet you couldn't do it."

"We made it." Thel swung into his saddle. Mountain climbing made him appreciate his horses even more.

"You'll have to try it, Ossie," said "Gene" Marston. "You can see everything for a hundred miles."

"I don't want to see anythin' that far off. What the hell good is it?" Despite his words, Ossie was more impressed with their feat than he wanted to admit.

When they rode into camp Thel noticed some big moose antlers hooked in a tree limb. "Hey! They got a good one!"

"That's the only nice thing about the bugger," said Ossie. "They brought in the back strap and it tasted awful. That bull must have been eatin' bearberries."

Ossie added that the two hunters had encountered the same Indian hunting party they had found above the Wind River. Tyghee had traded them the moose carcass for an armload of jerky. And now he and Henry Marston were out stalking antelope.

When the pair rode into camp that evening each had a buck antelope tied behind his saddle. "Aha!" cried Marston. "The alpinists have returned. Don't tell me—I can see it on your faces. You made it. I thought you would. Well, Eugene, this Riley is a remarkable guide, isn't he?" The cold look he gave his son belied his hearty words.

"Gene was the first one on top, Mr. Marston," said Thel.

The older man looked at his son in disbelief. "You! I certainly hope you left a cairn of rocks up there to mark your accomplishment. I daresay you're the first to climb that mountain."

"I was going to leave a cigar butt," said Eugene. "But the wind blew it over the edge."

"Don't be silly, Eugene," said his father. "What proof have you that you actually climbed the mountain? By Gad, people should know that a Marston was the first to climb that peak."

"I know it," said Eugene. "And Thel knows it."

"You wasted too much time studying philosophy in

school," said H. B. Marston. "Oh, hell; I'm glad you did it. Perhaps I should climb one of these mountains myself."

Thel groaned. "No, sir—one mountain per trip. Your son likes it a lot more than I do. We've got a lot of huntin' to do. We're gonna need every day."

At supper there was much good humor. It marked a pleasant change from the way Thel's guests had behaved since Eugene got drunk on the Gros Ventre. Thel hoped that now they would enjoy their trip and go back to Boston with a decent bag.

Unfortunately Thel's period of calm ended quickly. Tyghee came to him after the Marstons turned in. He reported a good hunt. The old father was a fine shot despite being bossy and muleheaded. But Tyghee was uneasy about the Indian hunting party. The four men suspected of murdering Viro Pocket were still with the group.

Clearly the Army at Fort Washakie wasn't making any progress on the case. And John Gurney had told Thel that detachments from the Yellowstone garrison were rarely seen in Jackson's Hole. It was Gurney's opinion that no more troops would patrol into the valley that year.

Thel said, "Those birds are being pretty cagey. They haven't made a move in our direction." He looked at Tige lying beside Ossie. "Maybe that dog's helpin' to keep 'em away." His words didn't carry much conviction. Those Indians bothered him.

In the morning they broke camp and started the long trek to the Upper Yellowstone. The game now was elk and grizzly bears. Perhaps Henry Marston would also find his rogue bull buffalo.

The horses had gorged on the rich grasses along the Snake River. Thanks to the good grazing and splendid fall weather, the animals were high-spirited. It took men and animals some time to settle down and pick up the rhythm of the pack train.

Late that afternoon they camped on the wild shores of Jackson's Lake. Henry Marston amused himself by fishing while his son rested. He was suffering the combined effects of travel, mountain climbing, and having had two fights in one week.

Once the horses were cared for, Thel asked Tyghee's opinion on their route. The Indian suggested turning due east to the Buffalo Fork country. After a day's ride they could turn north on the old trail to the upper Yellowstone River. In the vast meadows and surrounding timber they should find elk, grizzly, black bear and, possibly, buffalo.

The ride was uneventful. Eugene slumped in his saddle while his father was constantly on the lookout for game. In the late afternoon Tyghee showed them a campsite in the aspens beside a creek. While the tents were being pitched the hunters were serenaded by a bugling bull elk.

The next morning, as the party headed north, more bugling was heard. Henry Marston complained that they were passing by too many elk. Thel reassured him, saying there were plenty of elk farther north. The Thorofare, he said, harbored some of the largest bulls in Wyoming.

It was a tiring journey of twenty-five miles to the Upper Yellowstone. En route the party crossed the Continental Divide at Two-Ocean Pass. Here the waters of a creek divided, some flowing west toward the Pacific, the rest east to the Atlantic.

The first sight of the vast Yellowstone meadows thrilled the Marstons. Henry Marston exclaimed, "Superb!" He turned his horse onto a rise, the better to see this vast grassland. He waved Thel and Eugene to his side.

"Look," said Thel, "up there to the north. There must be fifty elk grazing."

Even Ossie's spirits got a lift when he saw the meadows. Tyghee led them across the great clearing. He often had to veer away from boggy ground. It took them a half hour to reach the river.

The Yellowstone meandered over a dark bottom. The water was so clear that it was difficult to judge its depth. Tyghee knew the fords, however. They soon left the river behind and took a campsite where there was firewood and good grazing nearby.

For Ossie it was a matter of pride to be able to call out,

"Hot water! Tea and coffee," within twenty minutes of unpacking.

The Marstons hurried to the fireside and accepted steaming cups of tea. "Thank you, Ossie," said Marston. "I believe your tea is served with more dispatch than at my club in Boston."

"I serve it with canned cow and sugar," said Ossie with a petulant smile.

Ossie broiled the last of the elk steaks for supper. In the morning, after the hunters left, he planned to find a fat cow elk and shoot her for the larder.

The Marstons turned in after supper. Thel and his two hands tidied the camp. Then they took a last look at the grazing horses and mules and went to bed themselves.

A few miles to the east there was another, simpler camp. The only shelter was a ragged canvas fly that covered a community bed of evergreen boughs and animal skins. There were four hunters sitting cross-legged around the fire. They were eating slivers of elk meat that each man cut for himself from a haunch roasting beside the fire.

One of the men, a swarthy fellow with long black hair, had a vivid scar on his right cheek. He was, of course, "Scar," the leader of the hunters who had taken Marston's bear. They were the same furtive men who had been hunting with Bead's band on Wind River.

Now they were hunting alone, taking elk skins and tusks to sell to the traders. As the men ate, they discussed the day's events. No elk had been shot but they had killed a lynx. Its pelt was stretched and pegged on the ground beside them.

The men had only two firearms. One was a smooth-bore musket. The other was a Sharps carbine. This weapon had been taken during a raid near Fort Fetterman ten years earlier. Its stock had been decorated with brass tacks and a medicine bundle hung from its muzzle.

The lynx had been shot with this carbine. The range was one hundred and fifty paces, twice the killing range of the old musket. A white hunter might have ridiculed the old

Sharps, but the Indians considered it their "medicine rifle" and handled it with reverence.

These men had quarreled repeatedly with Bead about the hunting grounds chosen and the division of meat and hides. Eventually, after consultation with their medicine bundles, the four companions struck out on their own. Each man believed this was the right decision.

A bright half moon was rising and illuminating the meadows with bluish light. Thel awakened and looked out of the tent. He saw silvery frost forming on the nodding grasses.

By morning a heavy rime of frost covered everything. When the sun came up it struck the meadows with blinding radiance. Thel and Eugene had difficulty spotting the elk that grazed near the timber. The animals saw them first and ran.

Tyghee and Henry Marston had similar luck. They had ridden east, following the Thorofare Creek. The stream meandered through timbered hills that were interspersed with wet meadows and brushy bottoms. As they prepared to ford the creek Tyghee saw a bull elk on the far bank.

It was a fine bull with wide, symmetrical antlers, six points to a side. The antlers' ivory tips flashed as the bull turned and trotted back into the trees. Tyghee motioned for Marston to follow him. They would try stalking on foot.

The elk's big cloven-hoof prints were easy to see in the hard frost. Tyghee followed them at a half trot. Although he was puffing, Marston kept up.

The bull entered heavier timber with many blow-downs. The stalkers were forced to slow down. The elk could jump the jack-strawed trees but the men had to struggle over and under them. Nevertheless Tyghee tracked the elk through the timber and to the edge of a meadow. It was misty in the meadow and the mist had darker threads of smoke running through it.

A few minutes earlier the elk had also stopped on the edge of the meadow. He turned his head to assess the danger. All his senses were concentrated on the back trail.

At the same moment Henry Marston ducked under a half-fallen tree. His hat touched a twig on the tree's underside and snapped it off. To Tyghee the noise sounded like a pistol shot. He tried to ignore it. These red-faced white men were so clumsy!

The bull heard the twig snap and with a bound stood in the meadow. He stopped there. The smell of smoke burned in his nostrils. He plunged back into the timber, fleeing both the smoke and the noisy hunter.

But when he reentered the woods, the elk also made a noise. A man lying beside the fire heard it. He sprang to his feet, snapping his fingers at his companions as he did so. The men looked just in time to see the elk trotting away through the trees.

It was a fine bull and sure to have handsome tusks. The Indians were still standing and discussing what to do about the elk when Tyghee and Marston reached the meadow's edge.

Tyghee reached out and stopped Marston before he blundered into the clearing. Silently the Indian pointed to the four figures grouped on the far side of the meadow. Marston tucked his rifle into the crook of his arm and uncased his field glasses.

The men were facing away, looking after the elk. Two of them wore flat-crowned hats with crimson bands. They were mixed bloods. The other two were blanket Indians with long hair and tattered buckskin shirts. As Marston examined the men, one turned and revealed his face.

Marston gasped. It was the scar-faced fellow who had ridden so brazenly into their camp so many weeks before. The Indians began to move. As each one turned, Marston recognized them. Marston's heart began to pound: these were the men who had murdered Viro Pocket!

Marston checked his Winchester. It was the repeater that held eight fat cartridges in its magazine. When he hefted that rifle, Marston welcomed the showdown that he knew would come. He knew the Indians' weapons were much inferior to the repeating rifles he and Tyghee carried. If only Eugene were here to take on these murderers with him!

Marston pulled Tyghee close to him. With signs and whispers he told the guide that these were the white man's killers. Tyghee did not need instruction. He also recognized the four hunters. He considered them thieves and renegades. They had disgraced their people and their great chief, Washakie. He would help the white man kill them.

CHAPTER TWELVE

THE FOUR INDIANS WERE STARTLED WHEN TYGHEE emerged from the woods and walked toward them. But he came with his right hand raised in a gesture of friendship and their alarm eased. The Indians recognized Tyghee. He was a famed hunter.

As Tyghee approached and held the Indians' attention, Henry Marston was slipping through the timber to get behind them. The scheme was for Tyghee to hold their attention until Marston got into position. Once he had them covered the Indians would be ordered to drop their weapons and surrender.

But the plan had a disastrous flaw. Henry Marston could never have slipped up and surprised an Indian. Before he got into position he stepped on a twig. It snapped. He immediately stopped and aimed his Winchester at Scar.

The Indians heard him and whirled to discover what was behind them. Seeing Marston half hidden in the woods and aiming a rifle, the Indians prepared to fight.

Tyghee immediately shot the man carrying the musket. Scar was trying to cock the old Sharps when Marston shot him. He dropped beside the man Tyghee had killed.

The other two hunters began to run. They had no guns but one carried a bow and some arrows.

Marston cried out, "Halt!"

The Indians ignored him, running as fast as they could toward the woods. Firing together, Tyghee and Marston both shot the unarmed hunter. He spilled headlong into the yellow grass, the back and sides of his buckskins dark with blood. The man was dead but when his body began twitching Tyghee shot him again.

Marston called out to the fourth man, "Halt!" He was a mixed blood and understood little English. He ignored Marston's command and raced for his life toward the sheltering forest.

Marston took a quick but deliberate aim. His bullet overtook the Indian in mid-stride. It entered at one hip and exited at the lower abdomen, leaving a hole two inches in diameter. The man fell into some low bushes. Although badly wounded, he was able to crawl into the woods. Marston fired at him again but missed.

Still clinging to his bow and arrows, the blood dragged himself farther into the timber. He heard the heavy footfalls of Tyghee and Marston running after him. Summoning his last reserves of strength, the blood pulled himself under a tangle of deadfalls and broken branches. Once inside the tangle, he rolled over on his back and nocked an arrow in his bowstring.

As they reached the trees, Tyghee grabbed Marston's arm and stopped him. Marston nodded. They both assumed their wounded quarry would come to bay and fight like a trapped animal. They expected an ambush.

The blood's tracks were plain in the forest duff. Tyghee moved a few paces off the tracks. He motioned to Marston to do likewise but in the other direction. It was dangerous to march straight down the track of a cornered enemy.

The pursuers advanced cautiously. Even at a distance it was easy to follow the man. His blood still gleamed on the ground and showed as bright red speckles on the green leaves of the undergrowth. The trail led into a jumble of half-fallen trees broken and jammed helter-skelter among the standing timber.

Tyghee inched forward, his moccasins making no sound. Marston advanced as quietly as he could. Under his new tan his face was rigid. His eyes were wide with excitement.

To him, it was like tracking the black bear. He glanced at Tyghee. The guide was intent on the forest tangle ahead. They must be nearly stepping on the blood, yet Marston could not see him. Suddenly Tyghee stopped and threw his rifle to his shoulder.

Marston also stopped and brought up his weapon. Tyghee barked a command in Shoshone. There was no reply. Tyghee waited a few seconds, then fired a shot into the tangle of broken trees and branches.

As Tyghee levered the spent shell from his rifle, the blood pulled himself erect. He had been waiting for this instant. His bow was raised, the arrow set against the taut bowstring. He would take Tyghee with him to paradise before the guide could shoot again.

Later Marston would remember it as a miracle that the blood stood at all. But his mind was numbed by shock and the loss of blood. He had forgotten Marston.

As the man stood and prepared to shoot Tyghee with his bow and arrow, Marston squeezed the trigger of his Winchester. The heavy .45-caliber slug struck the Indian in the side of his head. It was like shooting a ripe pumpkin at point-blank range.

Even Tyghee was shaken by the enormity of the man's head wound. After the first glance Marston would not look at it again. He had Tyghee drag the corpse from the woods while he went ahead, carrying the two rifles.

The dead hunters were dragged back to their camp and laid out side by side. Tyghee wanted to scalp Scar but Marston stopped him.

"No! These men must be taken to the garrison commander at Mammoth Hot Springs. The law is taking its course. You must learn, there shall be no scalping."

The pair returned immediately to their camp to await the return of Riley and Gene Marston. Ossie cooked them a meal. Tyghee ate his with relish but Marston had no appetite.

He told Ossie, "They were murdering thieves. Thank God we caught them before they killed again. But the whole affair has left me a little sick to my stomach."

Henry Marston had not seen men killed since the war and that was over twenty years earlier. Today, the fury and viciousness of battle returned to him as a ghastly memory.

But even as Henry Marston sat dull-eyed and drained of emotion an ember of pride was glowing within him. They had done it and he felt the credit was mostly his. They had destroyed a dangerous and brutal enemy.

Marston began jotting in a small notebook. He wanted to fix the particulars of the shooting in his mind. When he reported the incident to the Army he would be correct in every detail. As he wrote, however, he left out several facts.

He didn't mention that only two of the Indians had firearms—and old single-shots at that. One man was unarmed. The Indians had not threatened them and never fired a shot in their own defense.

What Marston had in the back of his mind as he wrote was the mutilated corpse of Viro Pocket. He saw again the dark faces of the four hunters. They were ugly with furtive eyes and long, greasy hair. Marston was eager to tell all of this to Riley and then to the military commander of Yellowstone Park.

But Riley and Eugene Marston did not return until after dark. They had spent the afternoon stalking a magnificent bull elk.

"A seven-pointer," Riley said, swinging down from his horse. "We got up on him twice but never had a shot." Riley was still excited.

He asked Marston who sat quietly beside the fire, "How did you boys do?"

"We got four," said the sportsman.

Riley was about to protest when Marston explained. "We found those fellows who murdered the sheepherder. I ordered them to surrender. They refused and prepared to fight. Tyghee shot the first one. He's the man to have on your side in a skirmish."

Riley interrupted, "Are you saying you took those fellows, just the two of you?"

"We killed them, Riley. I was using my lever gun. I never missed. Tyghee shot the first. I shot the second, the ugly one with the scarred face. We both hit the third fellow when he tried to run. Tyghee tracked the fourth killer in the woods. He tried to shoot Tyghee with his bow and arrow. I shot him, too." Marston did not elaborate on his shooting of the last man.

Riley silently thought this over. Then he asked Tyghee to tell him what had happened. The guide reported in detail. His account paralleled Marston's except that Tyghee said he was proud to have triumphed in battle.

Riley sat by the fire, thinking and smoking a cigarette. Finally he spoke, "The bloods were renegades. Who knows where they dropped from? The two Shoshones were on the outs with Washakie. He wanted them rubbed out. He'll be pleased but their relatives won't be. There will be some hard feelings.

"I think we should go out there first thing tomorrow and bury those fellows. You've done everyone a favor. But let's settle it quick and without a lot of talk."

"Riley!" Henry Marston was shocked. "If we do that we'll be as bad as those murderers. This must be reported. Justice has been done and we must have the sanction of the law. I forbid you to cover this up."

"Mr. Marston," said Thel, "back East you'd be right. But out West, some of us are still livin' by a different code. If we stir this up it will only cause more trouble. In a few years I'll let it be known what happened, naming no names. Justice will be done."

"Riley, I won't be moved on this," said Henry Marston. "We must observe the law."

"I agree," said Eugene. "That man's body was the most horrible thing I've ever seen. Father and Tyghee were right. Now they should do the right thing by the law."

Riley surrendered. To him the law and justice were two different things. The lawyers he had seen come west were scum. Slick scum, though, who used the law to line their pockets and the pockets of their clients. Justice had been done out there in the woods. Letting the law in on this was just going to mean trouble. He knew Eugene wanted to do the right thing. His father did, too. But Henry Marston also wanted to be able to tell people about what he had done.

"OK. We'll collect 'em first thing in the mornin'," said Thel. "Ossie, you and Tyghee start breakin' camp after breakfast. It's a long push from here to Mammoth. Some of it's rough trail. I hope it don't turn warm before we get those bodies handed in." For a hunting trip that had begun so smoothly, Thel thought, this one had sure gone to hell.

Congress had established Yellowstone Park in 1872. From the outset there had been serious problems. Some administrators had been corrupt, others incompetent. Congress refused to appropriate enough money to run the park. It became a haven for shifty characters. Many early-day travelers did not visit the park so much as they attacked it, defacing and destroying its wonders. Intermixed with this troublesome group was a shadowy skein of poachers, thieves, and gunmen.

In 1886 the U.S. Cavalry was officially put in charge of Yellowstone Park. But it was to take years before the Army got things under control. In 1887 most of the vast area had yet to see a soldier. In fact, without help from old-time hunters, the Army would have spent a lot of its time getting lost. Thel dreaded getting the Army involved in the shooting of the Indians.

He was up before daylight bringing in stock and making ready to move. The light came slowly. A heavy overcast covered the sky. There was an added chill in the ordinarily fresh breezes. When Thel and Mr. Marston left camp a few snowflakes were falling.

"Perhaps it is better that we move toward civilization," said Marston. "I wouldn't want to spend a winter in this wilderness."

"You won't," said Thel. "But you might like it better than wintering in Boston. I doubt it's gonna snow us in."

The four corpses lay where Tyghee left them. A flutter of gray-and-white camp robbers flew up as the men approached. The birds alighted on the limbs of nearby trees. They had been at the eyes and bullet wounds first. Their sharp beaks had multiplied the damage.

After tying the horses, Thel adjusted the packsaddles and tightened cinches. From the Indians' camp he took blankets and robes with which he wrapped the bodies. The bodies were awkward to handle.

While Riley loaded corpses, Marston poked through the camp. Riley suggested he look for things that had belonged to Viro Pocket.

A search of the bodies produced a few American and British coins. But they found none of the currency Eugene had used to buy the dog.

"A thieving Injun will take about anything," said Thel. "See if there's any gear from the sheep camp—maybe an ax or a knife. And look for his rifle. Remember, Viro had that little .32 rimfire. If we could show that, there wouldn't be any question."

But nothing was found that might have linked the Indians with the sheepherder's murder.

"They probably got rid of their loot weeks ago," said Marston. "I'm confident our testimony, combined with that of Captain Speer at Fort Washakie, will be all that's needed for proof."

Thel shrugged. He would have felt more comfortable if they'd found Viro's gun.

Their hunting camp was packed and gone by the time Thel and Marston returned to the site. Tyghee and Ossie had been watching the sky, too. Leaden clouds were hiding the surrounding peaks. It would be snowing by evening.

Thel did not anticipate a bad storm. The weather had changed too quickly for that. But it might snow six inches to a foot. He disliked to be packing out now, instead of snugging down in a warm, dry camp.

Tyghee had spent years roaming this wild region. He led

the way north, choosing a route that led along the east shore of Yellowstone Lake. They passed through some fine meadows on their way. There was always a chance they would see game.

Tyghee was oblivious of the order prohibiting hunting in the park. He had made many great hunts in this region. He refused to believe he now had to stop. Let the white man stop, not Tyghee.

He and Ossie set camp early. The tents were pitched and the horses were all staked and grazing when Thel and Marston arrived. Tyghee helped Thel unload the bodies and lay them under a tree. A canvas was spread over them as protection from weather and hungry predators.

As the two men walked to the tents, Tige came bounding to meet them. Everyone had become attached to this dog. Marston admired his courage and looked forward to showing him off back East. Thel valued the dog's intelligence and doubted the civilized East was a proper home for such an animal.

He stooped to give the dog's ear a gentle rub. "You stay out of the morgue, Tige." The dog had given the wrapped corpses a curious sniff but thereafter avoided them.

Everyone was tired and turned in soon after supper. It was a black night and silent except for the rustle of wind. Thel was awakened in the middle of the night. Tige was barking furiously. Ossie snored through it but Tyghee was sitting up in his blankets and smoking a cigarette.

"I'll take a look," said Thel. "That dog doesn't bark for nothing."

When Riley pushed back the tent flap he was met by a shower of snow. The air was filled with falling flakes and six inches had already accumulated on the ground. Thel called the dog and had him come inside the tent.

"Snow," said Thel, sliding back down in his blankets.

Tyghee grunted and Tige lay with his muzzle on his paws and growled softly. Thel only catnapped the rest of the night.

He arose at daylight and went out to find a foot of new snow. The snow had stopped but the sky was still leaden.

Below it the world was colorless, everything appeared either black or white. The horses stood humpbacked and sorrowful-looking in the meadow. Tige followed at Thel's heels as the guide shuffled through the snow, brushing it from the woodpile and rekindling the cooking fire. Periodically the dog stared into the surrounding forest and either barked or growled.

"What's in that timber, Tige?" Thel asked. "Is it a coyote or a bear?" When the fire was blazing Thel picked up the camp ax and went to where the corpses lay. Tige followed, growling.

Thel took one look at the place where the bodies had been, then ran back to his tent. Tyghee was standing outside.

Thel said, "A bear's been at those bodies. He dragged one of 'em off."

Reaching inside the tent, he grabbed his Winchester and levered a cartridge into the chamber. Tyghee had also armed himself and Riley signaled for him to accompany him. They did not see a bear but that didn't mean one wasn't close by.

They examined where the bear had been. It had thrown aside the canvas covering the bodies. With a forepaw it had turned over two of the corpses and selected a third which it dragged away.

The snow had partly covered the tracks. Tyghee knelt and blew the snow away, exposing a paw print. "Grizzly," said Tyghee. "Not too big."

"I thought it was," said Thel. He knelt beside Tyghee and, using his own hand for comparison, estimated the size of the bear's paw. As Tyghee said, it was not a big griz but it had a taste for human flesh.

"We got found by one bad bear," said Riley.

Tyghee nodded agreement. Then he waited for Thel's instructions.

"Let's follow the track awhile. Go ahead, Tige. Find him!" Riley waved the dog onto the bear's spoor.

His tail waving high in the air, Tige took the scent. Unlike many dogs, this one appeared to sense the danger. He did not run too far ahead of the men.

The bear went a quarter mile before stopping and beginning to tear at the corpse.

"Thunder, what a mess!" Riley turned away, disgusted.

Tyghee calmly examined the damage. "Him full now. Prob'ly go to sleep."

This was the season, prior to hibernation, when the bears were hungriest. Thel had known them to dig down through two feet of packed soil to unearth old carrion.

He said, "Marston can turn this in if he wants to. I say we throw some logs over it and leave what's left of him here. If we do that, maybe the bear won't come after the others."

In camp, Thel reported to the Marstons. Henry Marston was shocked. "You don't mean it? A bear *ate* that man? This is terrible!"

Thel replied, "A grizzly ain't learned manners, either. What's left of him isn't pretty. We are not gonna pack that mess all the way to Mammoth."

Marston protested. But when the guides showed him the corpse Marston nearly heaved.

When he could speak Marston said, "You're right. Bury it the best you can."

The remains were hastily covered with a few shovelfuls of dirt, then snow and tree limbs were thrown over that. In the meantime Ossie was breaking camp. That work went slowly. Tents and tarps had to be brushed clear of snow. Every bump under the white mantle had to be checked to be sure nothing was being left behind.

Once the party was on the trail they found travel slow, too. The riders were constantly hit by gobs of wet snow that plummeted from the branches overhead. The lead horses had to be rotated so no single animal was steadily breaking trail.

The lack of a clear trail to follow also delayed them. The party stopped shortly before dark.

Thel said, "We didn't make ten good miles today."

The Marstons were ready to stop. They were wet, tired and generally miserable. Eugene considered his chilled feet and soaking trousers. A glass of whiskey with some hot water, a cinnamon stick and brown sugar would have suited him. But he said nothing and tried to be agreeable.

Henry Marston vowed to erase the image of that ravaged corpse from his mind. That bear was a menace. Marston would enjoy emptying his rifle into that beast. He considered ordering Riley to return with him and destroy the animal.

This last thought alternated in Marston's mind with one of the orders he would give the park superintendent. "You can't allow such a creature to live in a public park!"

Riley looked inquiringly at Marston. "You talking to me?"

"Sorry, I was thinking about that bear. I must have been talking to myself."

CHAPTER THIRTEEN

THE MARK OF A GOOD TRAIL CREW IS IN THE WAY THEY care for the stock, pitch tents, and build fires in bad weather. A wet dude is often like a wet cat—mean and not much good for anything until it is dry. While Thel and Tyghee pitched tents, Ossie built a fire and put water on to boil. Thel led the Marstons into their tent and handed them their duffel.

He said, "You'll feel better once you get into dry clothes."

As he and his father stripped off their wet clothes, Eugene said, "I'd also like to get into a wet drink of whiskey."

His father stopped dressing and said angrily, "You'd better give that up, young man. Your damned booze won't help you steady a rifle."

Eugene didn't reply. He was shaking. He hadn't had a drink in over a week and he wasn't shaking from the cold.

While Tyghee staked the horses, Thel used his saddle horse to drag dry logs into camp. When he had cared for his

149

horse he began splitting the logs. While he worked, the Marstons appeared. They were warm and dry now. Ossie put steaming mugs of tea into their hands.

Marston stood watching Thel work. He said, "I think you, Eugene, and I should go back and take care of that bear."

Thel sunk his ax into a log. "I thought you wanted to turn the stiffs in at Mammoth? It could take a week to get that bear. And how would you know if you got the right one? There are a lot of grizzlies around here, but only one of 'em eats people."

Marston said, "I hadn't thought of that. You're right; we'll press on to Mammoth."

The sky began clearing. As the broken ridges of storm clouds passed overhead, a silvered moon rose in the sky. Its light shone coldly on the camp, making black shadows on the snow.

It also lighted the old camp, revealing the disturbed mantle of snow the hunters had left. There was no sound and just one creature in sight. A coyote was sniffing around for scraps.

The bear stood hidden in the shadows close to where the bodies had lain. He began sniffing around. The smell was strong but he could find nothing more to eat. He raised his head and looked at the coyote. In doing so he revealed the dished face and heavy muzzle of the male grizzly.

This was a huge bear. His face was scarred and twisted from many battles. Deep in the muscle of one hip lay the head of an arrow. The bear had almost forgotten the arrowhead but on nights like this when it was wet and cold his hip ached.

The bear curled his lips and "woofed." The coyote paused in mid-sniff, then bolted across the meadow, his bushy tail flapping behind him.

The bear ambled into the clearing. He too began sniffing around the abandoned camp. He found a scrap of leather that was salty with sweat and pungent with oil. He ate it. He ate potato peelings and some bits of half-charred food he found lying in the ashes. There was a strong smell of men all around but the bear ignored it. He found where bacon grease had been poured on the ground. He licked this hungrily, swallowing pine needles and dirt along with the grease.

The big grizzly had a heavy, dark coat intermixed with white hairs. Men called such bears silvertips. The bear carefully searched the campsite, but what he found only prodded his hunger. Eventually he gave up and shambled back into the timber.

As he walked, the arrow point in his hip jabbed at him. The bear growled at the pain. It was an old acquaintance. Years before, he had been crossing a divide and heading for the valley below. The valley was black with buffalo and it was calving season. He had come this way before. He was hungry and he knew the reddish newborn calves would be lying everywhere.

But as he crossed the divide a new smell reached him. It came from a pile of rocks near the trail. The bear "woofed" and stood erect to examine the rocks. As he did so the young Crow Indian who had been hiding there also rose.

This would be his first bear. He drew back the arrow in his bow and released it. It struck the bear in the side. The animal roared with pain and surprise. Then he turned and grabbed the arrow's shaft in his teeth. The wound was painful but not deep. The bear ripped the arrow from his side, crushed it in his jaws, and flung it aside.

As he did so the Crow shot a second arrow. But he was excited and his aim was hasty. This arrow struck the bear in the hip and penetrated deeply. The bear roared again and charged the Indian in his blind of rocks.

Until that moment the young man had envisioned himself arriving in camp with the head and pelt of a white bear. The women and children would crowd around him, chattering excitedly. The old men would come out of their lodges to see this young hunter whose heart was so strong.

But that was imagination and this was reality. The young man had never been charged by a bear. One of his last thoughts was how quickly the big animal moved. The bear threw himself on the blind, knocking rocks in all directions.

The Indian drew his bow a final time. But it was too late. The bear struck him with a forepaw. The arrow flew wildly at the sky and the broken bow clattered against the rocks.

The first blow had broken some of the man's ribs and knocked him over backward. With a savage roar the bear was on him, raking the Crow with his claws and biting at his face. The Indian struggled and reached for the knife at his waist.

As he grasped its handle the bear's fangs penetrated the Indian's braincase. There was a crunching sound and it was over. The bear rolled the body over, biting at it. Then the pain in his hip overcame his anger. He snapped at the embedded shaft and succeeded in grabbing it. When he pulled it, the shaft came free but the arrowhead remained embedded in the heavy muscle of the hip.

It was the first man the bear had ever seen and also the first one he ever killed. Few men dared to enter the region where this bear lived. Years sometimes passed without smelling their hated odor. As he grew old and wiser he came to avoid the source of that smell.

Now he was old and hungry. It was a long time since he had found buffalo calves scattered across the meadows. He had broken some of his teeth and those that weren't broken were worn and painful.

The bear moved up the trail to where the dead Shoshone lay. The place reeked with the scent of man. The Indian had been covered, but there was no covering his scent. It was easy to uncover him.

But the great bear stood back and only looked. Another bear was tearing at the remnants of the man. This was a much younger bear. He was not as large as the old bear but he was lean and powerful. He had killed a buffalo by breaking its thick neck with his huge jaws. Another time he had nearly decapitated a black bear that tried to share a kill with him.

The two bears had been traveling together since late summer. The old bear served as a guide and the young one had the strength and speed to feed them both. Separately they were grizzly bears, but together they were a combination from hell.

When the sun rose next morning it shone on a dazzling white landscape. Thel emerged from his tent stretching and working off the stiffness that had settled in his muscles overnight. Tyghee was already out catching horses and Ossie had coffee brewing and steaks frying.

"Mornin'," said Thel. "That meat smells good. We must be running low."

Ossie said, "I was gonna tell you, shoot the first meat you see. We got plenty of dried stuff and staples but we need fresh meat."

Thel replied, "The Army expects a man to feed himself. If the Marstons can get a nice bull elk and feed us at the same time, who's to complain?"

Tyghee came into camp leading several horses. Thel asked him about bears. Tyghee said there was no sign of a bear.

"Tige was quiet all night," said Thel. "I figure we've left the bears behind."

Tyghee nodded. But he had hunted many white bears. He respected them. Even if the bear wasn't seen for a week, that was no proof he wouldn't return.

Thel agreed. "We'll keep watch. Ossie, don't go wandering without a rifle. And pay attention to that dog. He'll tell us if anything's prowling around.

"Ossie says we're out of fresh meat. I think we should rest up here for a day. We can take the Marstons out and shoot an elk. It'll get them huntin' again and get us all some meat."

When the Marstons appeared they readily agreed to hunt elk for a day. Gene was not an enthusiastic hunter but he enjoyed being out with both Thel and Tyghee. It was agreed that while these four went hunting Ossie would dry equipment and do some chores.

Ossie Adams was fifty-five years old. He looked nearer sixty-five. He had fought in the Civil War and been decorated for bravery. But the politicians' promises for peace and Reconstruction were never kept to Ossie.

He had moved West reluctantly, borne along on a tide of fortune seekers. He drank. At first he drank because he wanted to. Later he drank because he had to.

Booze nearly finished Ossie. He believed that Thel Riley had appeared to save his life. He still slipped and got drunk, but he didn't stay drunk anymore. In bad times he hated Thel for keeping him alive, but most of the time he loved him. Thel Riley was the only human being in the world that Ossie Adams liked.

Ossie puttered around camp all morning. He made small repairs on the tack and dried out the tents and canvas tarps. He spread damp clothes and boots in front of the fire, being careful not to scorch them. He got the evening meal ready. All he had to do was put the Dutch ovens in the coals.

By late afternoon he was looking for something else to do. As he stood surveying the camp he heard a faint call. Soon that call multiplied and the sound increased. Ossie scanned the sky. When he first saw them they were just specks in the sky. But as he watched they grew larger. "Honkers," thought Ossie.

The birds were flying in formation and coming toward the camp. Ossie had seen Thel and Tyghee bring down high-flying geese with their rifles. He picked up his old single-shot and made sure it was loaded. If the geese flew over him he was going to have a shot.

But as Ossie waited, the V of birds began descending. They were still a half mile distant. They circled the meadow, skimming the tops of the trees. As Ossie watched, the birds set their wings and disappeared below the treetops.

"Damn," he said.

The geese had landed on a pond at the edge of the timber. The birds "talked" noisily as they paddled around. A goose dinner would be a treat for everyone. Thel was especially fond of roast goose. Ossie decided that he might move through the trees quietly and get a shot at the birds. He felt sure of bagging one goose, and if he was lucky he might get two. Tige could retrieve the birds for him.

So, shoving some extra cartridges into his pocket, Ossie set out for the pond with Tige beside him. The snow in the meadow was melting so Ossie kept to the shaded woods, trying to keep his feet dry. As they approached the pond the geese were feeding and "chatting" amiably.

Tige growled. Ossie tapped him on top of the head. "No!" he hissed. The dog would frighten off the birds before he had his shot. Tige continued to growl and Ossie slapped him. The dog reduced his growl to the softest of murmurs but he would not be quiet.

Ossie saw the pond through the scattering of trees. A dozen Canada geese were on the water. Ossie crouched low and began the final stalk that would bring him within range. Except for Tige's mutterings they slipped through the trees without a sound.

Ossie held his rifle ready. He had chosen the bird he wanted—a big fellow swimming near the far shore. A few more steps and he would be in position.

But Tige suddenly sprang forward, barking wildly. The geese panicked and amidst wild honking and beating of wings, they took wing.

"Tige, you son of—" The curse died on Ossie's lips, for standing before him not twenty feet away was a gigantic grizzly bear. He had risen onto his hind feet when the dog rushed at him. Ossie saw the bear's great yellow fangs as he roared a warning at the dog. Ossie, not wanting to repeat Viro Pocket's mistake of wounding a dangerous bear, fired his rifle into the air.

"Tige!" he called. "Come back!" Ossie fumbled for another cartridge in his pocket, then slipped it into the rifle. As he backed away from the bear he fired again and called the dog.

This time the dog obeyed. After making a last rush at the grizzly, Tige turned and trotted back to Ossie. The bear had not moved. He settled back onto four feet and growled at the retreating man and dog.

Ossie began to calm down. That was undoubtedly the largest bear he had ever seen. He reloaded the rifle with his last cartridge and, with the dog following, turned and began trotting away. As he ran he looked repeatedly over his shoulder to be sure the bear wasn't after him.

Tige ran to Ossie, then began barking again. The dog rushed ahead. The hackles on his back were erect and his tail was poker-stiff. Then the young grizzly lunged from behind some thick evergreens.

Tige flew at him barking and snarling. Ossie could hear the dog's teeth snapping. He raised his rifle, calling off the dog at the same time.

Ossie hesitated. The young grizzly was only twenty-five feet away. He could see the hair standing on the bear's shoulders and the small black eyes set in the snarling face. Tige seemed to sense that this was the most dangerous bear he had ever faced. He also sensed that he had come too close. When the bear charged, Tige tried to dodge out of his path.

The bear hit Tige with a forepaw and slammed him into a tree. The dog howled with pain and tried to limp away as the bear grabbed him. He gripped Tige between his huge paws and pulled the struggling dog toward him.

Ossie fired. The slug ripped across the bridge of the bear's muzzle, then tore out his right eye and part of the socket. The animal roared in agony. In a frenzy he bit Tige, crushing his skull. Then he charged Ossie.

Ossie tried to run, stumbled and nearly fell. He recovered and leaped at a young spruce. Ossie clawed at the branches, his legs kicking frantically as he tried to climb the tree. But the thin branches snapped as he pulled at them. He clawed at the tree, his heart pounding in terror. He was only three feet off the ground when the bear caught him.

The grizzly's terrible roaring never stopped even as he grabbed Ossie's ankle and dragged him from the tree. The man's scream mingled with the enraged roaring of the bear. The bear hit Ossie with his forepaw. There was a sharp snap. He had broken Ossie's neck.

The bear shook Ossie's limp body like a dog shaking a rag doll. When there was no response he flung the body aside. The grizzly sat down and pawed at his eye. He was in agony from the wound. But pawing only aggravated the injury. The bear's face and chest became smeared with blood. He rolled on the ground, rubbing his face into the dirt.

But there was no relief from the excruciating pain. The bear got up and began running. He ran wildly, banging into trees and smashing against deadfalls. Using his forepaws he battered anything that stood in his way. In his fury he bit poles and tree limbs in two.

The bear only stopped running to roll and rub his face against the ground. The dirt and forest duff that stuck to the wound and blood-soaked fur made the animal more hideous than ever. But the dirt also stemmed the flow of blood. When the animal had gone nearly ten miles he began to tire. The shock of being wounded was weighing him down.

The bear came to a toppled spruce. A large pit remained where the roots had been. Growling and muttering to himself, the grizzly crawled into this pit and lay down.

The old bear had not moved when Tige rushed the younger grizzly. He watched the dog and then Ossie being killed. The other bear had gone beserk and run away. The old bear understood that he must now avoid the younger bear.

He waited for a few minutes, listening and sniffing the air. Then he went to where Ossie lay and smelled him. He rolled the corpse over and pawed at it. Then he went to where the dog lay. Most of Tige's bones were broken and the bloody carcass was draped limply over a log. Without hesitation the old grizzly ate Tige. He left nothing but a few hairs and some pinkish bloodstains on the snow. Then he shambled back into the timber, lay down beside a log and fell asleep.

The hunters did not return to camp until after dark. Henry Marston had killed a large bull elk. Thel had dressed and butchered it, leaving the hide intact between the quarters but separating the front from the back quarters. With Marston's help he slung the hindquarters, hair side down, across his saddle.

They were still well out from camp when they saw the

flickers of the campfire. Thel said, "Looks like supper will be ready when we get there."

"I don't know what you'd do without Ossie," said Marston. He was anticipating having a mug of hot coffee put in his hand.

Tyghee and Eugene were seated by the fire when Thel walked into its light. "Hi, boys," he said. "Have any luck?"

"Ossie isn't here," said Eugene. "The dog's gone, too."

"That's funny," said Thel. "Did you see his tracks?"

Tyghee said Ossie and the dog had gone down the meadow, walking in the edge of the woods. It was too dark to follow him farther, so Tyghee returned and put Ossie's Dutch ovens in the fire.

The Indian helped Thel to unload the elk quarters and care for the horses. When the animals were staked in the meadow and grazing, Thel called, "Ossie! Tige! Here!" There was no response.

Thel said, "Let's eat. If the old boy's lost he'll sit down and wait for us. If he doesn't show up by the time we've eaten, I'll fire some shots."

Thel tried to remain calm. But this was not like Ossie. If he had become lost the dog could lead him back to camp no matter how dark it was. Thel filled his plate from the Dutch ovens but only toyed with the food.

He asked Tyghee, "He took that old rifle of his, didn't he?"

Tyghee said the rifle was gone. He added that he could make pitch-wood torches and track the missing man.

Thel nodded. "Let me shoot first. We'll give him a few minutes."

There was no reply to Thel's shots. He said, "Let's go take a look." He asked the Indian if he thought the grizzly had followed them, but Tyghee could only shrug. Who could say what a white bear would do? Especially now, with their long winter sleep approaching.

Leaving the Marstons in camp, Thel and Tyghee set out. Ossie's tracks were easy to read. Tyghee followed them at a trot. But the light of the flickering torches restricted the tracker. He could not look ahead or to the side and take shortcuts. Each footstep had to be traced.

Tyghee led them to the edge of the pond. He saw where Ossie had stopped. He picked up a fired cartridge case and handed it to Thel. Then he followed the dog's tracks to where he had encountered the old bear.

"Heap bear," Tyghee muttered as he quickly unraveled the turmoil he saw in the disturbed snow. He followed Ossie's footprints and found a second cartridge case. Then he found Ossie face down in the snow.

"Here!" called Tyghee.

Thel saw by the odd angle of Ossie's neck that it was broken. He knelt beside the body and put his hand on the older man's shoulder.

"Oh, damn that bear! Damn it to hell." Thel stood up, wiping his eyes. "Tyghee, we're gonna get that son of a bitch!"

Tyghee next found where Tige had been killed and eaten. In the eerie torchlight he discovered that there had been two bears. One had been wounded. Deliberately and with uncanny accuracy the guide showed Thel the signs and told him what had happened.

"You say it was the smaller bear killed him?"

Tyghee said yes. He could not be positive but he believed that the great bear had eaten the dog but not killed him. Tyghee also felt that the younger bear was the one that had dragged away the Indian's body.

"So there were two grizzlies traveling together," Thel was thinking aloud. "We're gonna' kill 'em both. I don't care how long it takes. To hell with Henry B. Marston. He's the cause of this." Thel knelt and lifted Ossie in his arms. Tyghee offered to help him but Thel wanted to carry Ossie by himself.

When he walked into camp he went directly to the fire circle and put Ossie down.

"My Lord!" said Henry Marston. "The man's dead. His neck's broken."

"Griz," said Thel. "Two of 'em. Tyghee and I are starting at daylight."

"We're with you, of course." Marston's outrage erupted. "Those bears must be destroyed."

Eugene thought his father was being self-righteous, but he also agreed to hunt down the bears. It would not be easy for him because he was afraid of those bears.

The men went to bed but no one slept. Even the implacable Tyghee sat up in his blankets most of the night and smoked cigarettes. To him the bears were no longer just wild animals but devils surrounded by evil spirits. He would track them down and kill them. Only after he had done that would his heart be strong again. Now he sat smoking and muttering an old death song.

Marston appeared next morning with a full cartridge belt around his waist and another fastened across his chest. Thel would have grinned at all the munitions if he had not been so sad.

They wrapped Ossie in a blanket and buried him in the edge of the woods. Thel placed large rocks on the body to discourage marauding animals.

When the grave was covered he said to Marston, "I'm hanging those three stiffs in the trees. We haven't got time to bury 'em. Besides, it's their way. Maybe we can turn 'em in later, maybe we can't. Either way, I'm through foolin' with 'em."

Marston merely nodded. His guide was upset and it would be unwise to antagonize him. The matter of the Indians could be taken care of later. He agreed that the first business was to eliminate the grizzlies.

Before the men left camp Thel handed out lunches saying, "Sorry, this ain't fixed the way Os would have done it. But it'll keep you, and we're in a hurry."

The search began at the killing site near the pond. The bear tracks led in almost opposite directions.

Thel said, "We'll split up. Tyghee and Mr. Marston will follow the big track. Gene, you and me will take the smaller one. He's wounded and probably ten times meaner than that black your father shot."

Before separating, the men agreed that whichever pair

found and killed their bear first would backtrack and help the other two hunters.

As they parted Thel said, "When you see hair, shoot. Pump that bastard so full of lead he can't move. This is killin', not huntin'."

Sufficient snow remained to afford easy tracking. Because the younger bear had left running, Thel tracked from the saddle. He hoped to overtake the bear as soon as possible.

The old grizzly had not run, but had stayed in the timber. Tyghee and Marston tracked him on foot. The bear had headed for some second-growth pine—some called it "dog-hair pine" because it was so thick. The horses had to be tied and left behind.

The two men hardly spoke. Tyghee preferred not to talk to this white man. And ever since the trip began he had let Marston think he didn't understand what Marston said. Like many Indians, Tyghee believed that one day soon the buffalo would return and the white men would disappear.

Chapter Fourteen

T HE OLD BEAR NATURALLY SOUGHT HIS BED IN THE THICK
second growth. When the younger bear went mad, attacking
everything in his path, the older bear had been alarmed. It
was the first time in his life that he had come close to being
afraid.

The second growth was so thick that Tyghee sometimes
dropped on all fours to track the bear. He moved very
slowly. They might not see the bear until he was just feet
away. Although there was no sign of blood, Tyghee had to
assume this animal might be wounded. It was vital that
Tyghee see the bear as soon as possible. If he didn't, the
bear might charge and be on him before there was time to
shoot.

The men crept forward, inspecting every inch of the
tangle ahead. Tyghee did not take another step until he was
sure he did not see the bear. Marston followed close behind.
The man was courageous. He carried his lever-action
Winchester loaded and at the ready. If the grizzly appeared,

all he had to do was thumb back the hammer, aim and fire. Marston also realized that there might be only a split second in which to stop the bear.

The grizzly had awakened at first light. His hip ached from his ancient wound. He growled then stood and stretched himself. As he did so he listened and put his thick snout in the air, sniffing.

There was little wind and what there was eddied and often changed directions. The bear scented nothing unusual. He was hungry again. He started for the place where he had eaten the dog.

The bear moved through the dog-hair pine more easily than the men. He followed his back trail from the previous evening. Suddenly he stopped. He had smelled something. He stood erect, sniffing and listening. The wind eddied, carrying the hunters' scent in another direction. The bear paused. Then he growled and moved off his back trail. He was going to circle instead of going straight back to the kill site.

The eddying wind made Tyghee uneasy. The gentlest of stray breezes could carry their scent to the bear. Tyghee advanced even more cautiously. Marston, in his ignorance, failed to consider wind currents he couldn't feel. He decided Tyghee was becoming frightened. The guide hardly moved at all.

Marston had seen men lose their nerve before. In battle, some soldiers became paralyzed with fear. They let enemy troops bayonet them where they stood without firing a shot. Marston saw that Tyghee was still tracking. But at this rate they would never find the bear.

Henry Marston decided that if they ever found the bear it would be up to him to kill it. The Indian might panic at the crucial moment. A man could not take any chances.

Soon Tyghee stopped altogether. He had smelled something. The tiniest hint of the fetid odor of an old boar grizzly. He waited, listening and sniffing. But the zephyr that had brought him the scent drifted away.

Marston became increasingly impatient. He glanced at his watch. *Good Lord!* he thought. *We have been crawling through this undergrowth for two hours.* He stood up. Branches scraped across his canvas coat.

Tyghee looked at Marston in astonishment. These crazy white men! With one hand he reached up and jerked Marston back down beside him. Then he pointed into the green and gray tangle of evergreen. He did not even whisper but his mouth formed the word, "Bear!"

The men waited, listening. Marston felt drops of sweat running down his back. His hands were clammy and his legs ached from squatting. When Marston doubted if he could wait another second, Tyghee moved. Marston sighed audibly and moved after him.

The old bear had also been waiting. He too had smelled something. He had scented men. When he heard Marston sigh, his muscles tensed and he growled. He saw a movement and charged.

"There he is!" Marston cried. The hunters were standing in a tangle of chest-high evergreens. In his frenzy to shoulder his rifle and fire, Marston shoved Tyghee aside. The Indian's feet tangled in the brush and he nearly fell. Out of the corner of his eye Tyghee saw the grizzly coming: ears back, jaws open and snapping.

Marston coolly put the bead of his front sight on the bear's nose and squeezed the trigger. There was a metallic "snap" that seemed so loud it overpowered the bear's roaring.

"Misfire!" In a panic Marston jerked the lever. He did not jerk it far enough, and when he closed the Winchester's breech the weapon jammed.

The grizzly was almost on them when Tyghee regained his feet. The old Winchester flew to his shoulder. Tyghee fired. The range was less than ten feet. The bear lunged forward, smashing the trees and knocking Marston down.

When Tyghee fired again the muzzle of his rifle was actually touching the bear's skull. The animal quivered, his legs twitching and jaws working. Marston fought his way out from under the collapsed trees. The grizzly's forelegs had been resting on his foot. Marston stood up and then sat down again. His legs were too wobbly to support him. His hands trembled uncontrollably.

Marston looked up at Tyghee. The Indian's dark face wore a wide grin. He was laughing at Martson and rolling a cigarette.

"Heap bear," he said.

Tyghee reached into his pocket and loaded two stubby .44/40 cartridges into his Winchester. Then he shouldered the rifle and set off to find the horses. His contempt for Marston at that moment was too great for him to be near the man.

Marston tried standing again. He took a deep breath and got his trembling under control. Then, still moving on rubbery legs, he bent to examine the bear.

He realized that by pushing Tyghee out of the way he had nearly gotten them both killed. Tyghee had saved them both in spite of Marston's panic-stricken stupidity.

The bear had been shot twice in the head. Tyghee's first bullet had landed where the guide wanted it to. The heavy slug had penetrated the bear's brain. The bear was dead when he landed in the brush where the men stood. But Tyghee took no chances and had put a second bullet into the bear's skull. Either shot would have been instantly fatal.

Later Marston would remember that moment. He tried to estimate the length of time it had taken Tyghee to raise his rifle, aim and fire. Surely it had been far less than a second. His shots came so close together a bystander could not have separated them.

Marston looked down at the great bear. It made the black bear they had shot look like a cub. And, for the first time, he admitted that while he had shot that bear it was Thel Riley who had killed it. He had to walk away. Looking at the grizzly was causing him to tremble again.

"Tyghee!" called Marston. "Wait for me. I'm coming!"

The Indian didn't stop until he was back with the horses. When the white man came stumbling up to him, Tyghee was tightening their cinches. He glanced at Marston but went on working.

"We find boss now." Tyghee handed Marston his reins, then vaulted easily into his own saddle.

"I'm sorry, Tyghee," Marston blurted. "My rifle misfired. You saved my life."

The Indian turned in his saddle and faced Marston. "No," he said. "Tyghee save Tyghee's life."

Since taking the younger grizzly's track Thel Riley had never slowed the pace. He paid scant attention to Eugene, who was fifty yards behind him and struggling to keep up. Thel's hunt was personal.

At last, after riding steadily for three hours, Thel reined in. Eugene caught up and asked, "Hasn't the bear ever stopped?"

"A few times to rub his head in the snow. He only stopped runnin' a couple miles back." Thel dismounted to rest his sweating horse.

"Do you have an idea where the bear is going?" asked Eugene.

"Nope. I've never been in this place before," Thel replied. "I think he's just runnin' crazy. Trying to get away from the hurt. He's walking now; we could find him anytime."

Thel was mistaken. The men were still tracking the bear that afternoon. It led them over ridges, through timbered canyons, crossing one divide and then another. Riley's pursuit was relentless.

They found the place where the bear had rested under the exposed roots of the fallen spruce. Thel examined the spot.

He said, "I don't think the bear's jaw is broken. Ossie must have shot an eye out or knocked a chunk out of his skull. A griz is the meanest thing walking. And one that's hurt like this must be the devil's own."

From where they stood resting, Thel looked far up the valley to where a steep cliff marked the divide. Up there, lying among the broken rocks and protected from the wind, was where he placed the bear.

"I have a hunch he stopped up there." Thel pointed to the

castle-like wall now glowing red in the late afternoon sunshine.

"How do you know?" Eugene thought the escarpment little different from several they had already seen.

"I know the same way the bear knew to go up there." Thel smiled for the first time since discovering Ossie.

Eugene was tired and obviously ready to return to camp. Thel was unsympathetic.

He said, "We're not givin' up on this bear. We'll sleep out tonight and maybe tomorrow night. I tracked a lion once for ten days. My horse gave out an' I had to turn him loose. Left my saddle hangin' in a tree. I was eatin' porcupines before that hunt was over."

The grizzly's track did lead toward the great escarpment. The higher the hunters climbed, the deeper they found the snow. When Thel finally stopped it was halfway to their knees.

He said, "He's stopped runnin'. And he's hungry. He stopped back there to lick grubs outta that old log."

"Perhaps we should wait for help," said Eugene.

Thel replied, "Ossie was my friend for a dozen years. I have a hunch he got killed huntin' some geese on that pond. If he'd gone after a bear he'd have borrowed one of the big rifles. Every trip he always got me a couple of geese. I climbed that damned mountain with you. Now stick with me and we'll get that bear."

"I wish I had a drink," said Eugene.

Thel snapped. "I wish I had somebody with me that was man enough to admit he had a problem he wouldn't face!"

Not another word was exchanged as the two men, climbing on foot now, toiled upward. They finally stopped a half mile below the escarpment.

Thel said, "This will be a cold camp. It's too dark to try for him now. Wrap up in your saddle blanket and burrow down in the snow."

Thel cut evergreen boughs and directed Eugene in making a bed and windbreak with them. While Eugene worked, Thel cut firewood. Then he fed the tired horses the small ration of grain he'd packed.

"Poor buggers," he said. Thel rubbed their matted backs with the grain sack to stimulate circulation. "A good rub helps keep 'em from getting sore."

The men sat by a flickering fire eating cold meat and biscuits. Eugene said little, and Riley did not encourage him. He wanted to be alert in case the bear turned around and came back down the valley.

In the meantime Tyghee and Henry Marston had also made a rough camp. The resourceful Tyghee had shot a deer. He showed Marston how to roast ribs over an open fire.

Marston found them delicious. "I didn't think meat this fresh was edible," he said, wiping his chin.

Tyghee just looked at him. To him meat was meat; you ate it when you had it. As a boy Tyghee had eaten buffalo brains raw and still warm from the animal. He thought whites had a lot of strange superstitions.

When they were both full and lying full length before their fire Marston said, "If the gentlemen in my club at home could just see me. They'll never believe this. Tyghee, can you read or write?"

Tyghee shrugged. He'd never thought about it. So Marston took a business card from an inner coat pocket. He held the card so Tyghee could see the printing on it. Tyghee took the card and ran a greasy finger under the words.

"That's me," said Marston pointing to himself.

Tyghee nodded. Then he turned the card over and with a blackened twig from the fire scratched a picture. Finished, he handed the card to Marston.

Pointing to the crude figure he had drawn he said, "Tyghee." Then he pointed to a second figure. It was the bear lying flat in the undergrowth. Tyghee had made marks showing where his bullets had struck it.

Marston studied it. "I see. Tyghee and the bear he killed today. I am not in the picture. You old heathen, we'll see who kills the next bear." Marston smiled but he was angry. How dare this illiterate Indian, practically a savage, criticize him!

Marston returned the card to Tyghee. "We had better get some rest. Tomorrow may be a long day."

Marston pulled his cap low, trying to protect his cold ears. He buttoned his coat tightly around his neck and covered himself with his saddle blanket. He was too tired to be offended by the smell of horses.

Thel and Eugene ran out of firewood before dawn. The cold that had earlier nipped at the men now bore down on them with a vengeance.

Eugene's teeth were chattering. "Give me the hatchet," he said, "I'll cut some more wood."

"Sit still," said Thel. "The griz might be out there, too. Hang on—the sun will be up soon."

Thel was cold too. He touched the Colt revolver and the Winchester lying beside him. The steel was so cold it seemed to burn his fingers. Thel put his hands under his armpits to warm them and fought to keep from shivering.

As the cold penetrated the rock cliffs above them, tiny contractions occurred. Occasionally a stone broke loose and clattered onto the talus below. The bear, still tortured by the searing pain in his head, got up and turned around. He had found a grassy niche under the tall cliff. He had even managed to catch and eat a small chipmunk as he lay there. He now had two drivers, pain and hunger.

He had smelled the wood smoke during the night and heard the noises of men. But finally both the sounds and the smell of men had ceased. The bear stood and rubbed his head against the inside of his foreleg.

This only aggravated his wound. The bear whirled and clubbed a cobble-sized rock that lay before him. The rock went spinning away, then bounded down to crash among the rocks below.

Thel reacted instantly. He picked up his revolver and cocked it.

"What is it?" asked Eugene.

"That rock. It made too much noise. Something knocked it loose." Riley sat in the darkness watching and listening.

He could just make out vague shadows against the bluish

snow. He eyed one shape for ten minutes before deciding it was a boulder and not a bear.

Then from the black wall of silence came a sound. It was a tree branch being bent and then swishing back into place. Riley strained to see in the darkness, but there were only dim shadows. All of them seemed to be moving.

There was a second sound—the grating of one pebble against another. Thel touched Eugene's shoulder.

He whispered, "He's out there. Cock your rifle."

Thel weighed the revolver in his hand then rested it on one knee. He wondered if he was choosing the right weapon? The Winchester was far more deadly, even at close quarters. But he could fan the Colt's hammer. Fanning wasn't accurate but it would fill a spit second with more flying lead and flashing thunder than two Winchesters. Thel was gambling it would turn, if not stop, the bear.

The hunters waited, crouching tensely in the darkness. From above them came a low growl that exploded into a roar. Eugene banged off two shots. Thel heard the bullets smack against distant rocks.

"Stop!" he ordered.

"I thought I saw something," said Eugene.

"You shoot when I do," said Thel. Now reload and stay ready."

He heard the soft scrape of the cartridges as Eugene pushed them into the magazine. There was a second scraping sound. Thel braced. He had heard one of the grizzly's claws scrape across a rock. In the next instant the grizzly charged, roaring out his pain and hatred.

Thel's revolver blazed like an exploding star in the darkness. The crashing gunfire and blinding flashes created a hellish scene. Thel glimpsed a big, shadowy form and then he smelled it.

Riley was hit. It was a stunning blow that sent him flying like a tenpin. The Colt was knocked from his hand and sent spinning. Thel landed hard on one shoulder. He lay quietly and drew his belt knife.

"Gene, where is he?"

From an explosion of deafening gunfire and insane

roaring a deathly silence had followed. Thel pulled himself into a crouch. In the gloom he saw Eugene standing rooted and still holding his rifle to his shoulder.

"Gene," said Thel. "I've dropped my gun. If he comes again you'll have to take him."

Eugene Marston did not reply but Thel heard him shoving fresh cartridges into the Winchester. Thel rested on one knee, moving his arms and hands and checking himself for injuries. Nothing broken or bleeding.

"He must have come between us," said Thel. "I got bowled over like I was bouncing off a locomotive. Don't shoot me, now. I'm standing up. Want to find my rifle."

Eugene finally spoke. "Where is he? Did we get him?"

"We hit him but I don't know if we *got* him. How many times did you shoot?" Thel asked.

Eugene was still rattled. "Let's see, I just put three shells into the magazine." He spoke slowly as if he were waking from a deep sleep.

Although he was not seriously hurt, Thel knew he would be sore for a week. He felt around and found his rifle.

He said, "That's nine shots. We must have hit him a few times. We'll have to wait. He'll either come back or we'll go find him after it's light."

Tyghee bolted upright when he heard the shooting. It came from far off, like a clap of distant thunder. He tossed wood on the fire and checked his rifle. He was apprehensive.

Henry Marston had not been able to sleep. He said, "They were shooting. I wonder if they got him?"

Tyghee took out his tobacco and rolled a cigarette. "We wait," he said.

In an hour the first light appeared as faint tracing behind the eastern peaks. As soon as he could see, Tyghee gathered their few possessions and saddled the horses. When he could see his rifle sights they set out.

Marston rode but Tyghee led the way on foot. If they met a wounded grizzly he might not have time to dismount.

Tyghee moved at deliberate speed; his every sense was straining to find the bear before it found him.

At dawn Riley and Eugene were also ready. Thel examined the grizzly's tracks. He was deciphering what had happened in the darkness.

"I guessed right," he said. "The bear came between us. And he's hit. We both hit him. There's blood on both sides of his tracks. I wish I knew how bad he's hit."

Before leaving Thel searched unsuccessfully for his revolver. "Damn. Guess I'd rather lose it than my rifle."

"Don't worry," said Eugene. "When we get back to camp I'll give you my pistol. I could never hit anything with it."

Thel remembered the gleaming weapon he had seen in the Marstons' private car back in Rawlins. It rested on red velvet in a fitted walnut case.

"That's mighty nice, Gene. I'll give you a chance to change your mind." Riley tugged on his horse's reins and set off walking down into the valley.

As Riley followed the bear's tracks he fervently hoped they would find it lying dead. But Riley knew his hopes seldom came true.

Although the bear was badly wounded they did not find it. The animal was either falling or lying down periodically. Thel showed Eugene the dark pools of blood it was leaving behind.

"He's hit hard," said Thel. "But he's so full of hell he could go ten miles on guts alone."

Eugene asked, "Do you think he'll try to attack us again?"

"He might. More'n one hunter has walked up on a dying grizzly and then died with him."

Far below the escarpment, where the valley leveled out, Thel saw a movement.

"Look there," he said. "It's Tyghee and your old man."

In twenty minutes the hunters met. Thel described the bear's attack.

Marston interrupted. "We were charged, too. But at least we could see. What did you think of it, Eugene? That kind of action cuts close to the bone, doesn't it?" Marston was over the fright he'd suffered the previous morning.

Eugene didn't share his enthusiasm. "I'd rather get my thrills climbing mountains. I never want an experience like that again." For Eugene the ascent of a mountain had been clean and exhilarating. But stopping the charge of a bear had been brutal and primitive.

Henry Marston's lips tightened to an angry white line. He glared at Eugene while the two guides conferred.

The tracks showed that the bear had left the valley and gone up a brushy draw. Tyghee made a sour face. Following wounded grizzlies into the brush was becoming a dangerous habit.

The horses were tied and the men began single-filing up the draw. Thel led. The place was a tangle of downed and half-fallen lodgepole pine. Tracking was both difficult and slow. By midafternoon the men had traveled only three hundred yards.

As the best tracker, Tyghee had taken the lead. In an hour the jackstrawed trees abruptly ended. They had reached an opening where there was grass surrounding some large fir trees.

Tyghee stopped. It was in such places that game was often found. He studied the clearing's far edge. There was a boulder at the base of a fir. Tyghee spotted something behind it. Thel came up and stood beside the Indian. He had seen it, too.

CHAPTER FIFTEEN

"I'S HIM!" SAID THEL, LOOKING TO HIS RIFLE.

Henry Marston pushed in beside the guides. "Have you found him? Where is he?"

Thel pointed out the object at the base of the boulder. It took him a while but Marston finally spotted it by using his field glasses. The object the guides had seen so easily with their naked eyes was the tip of a bear's paw.

Thel and Tyghee discussed the situation. Then Thel said to the Marstons, "This isn't a good spot. We can't be sure which way the bear's facing. He may have another charge left in him. Tyghee and I will split and work up on either side of him."

"What do we do?" asked Henry Marston.

"You stay here. If the bear shows, shoot him." Thel was playing this as safely as possible.

Henry Marston disagreed, saying, "I want Eugene in on

this kill. We've come a long way and spent a lot of money for a moment like this. Come on, son, let's give that damned bear a proper send-off."

Eugene shook his head. "Go ahead, Father. You enjoy this sort of thing."

Marston stepped forward and slapped his son across the face. His own features were twisted in rage. "Yellow! You sniveling little snot. I disown you! From now on you're no son of mine!"

Eugene stood rigidly before his father. His face was white but he made no reply.

Thel said, "C'mon, Mr. Marston, you follow Tyghee."

Leaving Eugene where he preferred to stay, the three divided and began working their way along opposite sides of the clearing. Tyghee kept one eye on the boulder and the other on Marston. He would not be pushed again if the bear charged.

When Riley flanked the rock he could see the bear clearly. The bear was lying on his belly with his rump to him. His head was resting on his forepaws. Thel remembered that Tige used to lie that way.

It was a bad angle for a shot. Thel aimed at the spine between the animal's hips. If the bear moved he could break it down. But from his position he could not be sure of making one, killing shot. He nodded to Tyghee who was now in position with Marston on the opposite side of the clearing.

Marston's voice was choked with excitement, "He's alive! See, he's looking right at us. I'll take him!"

Tyghee held out an arm delaying Marston. The bear was alive. It had been a magnificent animal with a light, almost blond coat that graded to rich brown on the shoulders and neck. He was not magnificent now. Half of his great dished face was shot away. His rich coat was dirty and soaked with blood.

Tyghee thought, "Old brother, this is your last time. My heart is sad for you. I must let this white man rub you out."

Almost as if he read Tyghee's thoughts, the bear raised his head and stared at the Indian with his one remaining eye. He uttered a low growl and Marston shot him in the face. The grizzly's head dropped onto his paws. From him came a long, almost gentle sigh.

Tyghee again had to stay Marston. They would wait while Tyghee smoked a cigarette. He wanted to be sure the bear was dead. When he had smoked his cigarette halfway down, Tyghee stuck it in his mouth and waved Thel forward.

The three men met and stood looking at the carcass. Marston said, "My God, he's an ugly devil! A man-eater!"

Thel did not reply. Even in death this bear had a wild majesty. He was ugly only because they had shot him to pieces. The guides rolled the bear onto his back and began skinning it.

Marston watched. He ignored Eugene when his son joined the group. Marston said, "We've done a service here. These bears have no place in a public park. It's just too bad that a man had to die before we killed the bears."

Eugene looked down at the skinned carcass. It resembled a man. He said, "It looks like that sheepherder when you showed me his body in the dispensary."

Thel had already noted the resemblance. But all he said was, "I was always after Ossie to get himself an express rifle. That peashooter of his let him down once too often."

Thel thought of Pocket. The sheepherder had also been armed with a weapon best suited for potting rabbits and butchering sheep. Why did men risk their lives to save a dollar on a cheap rifle? He recalled that Bischoff's crony, Snub, had also had such a rifle. Thel shrugged and went back to his skinning.

When they had finished, Tyghee wrapped the bear's skull inside the pelt. It was then bundled and carried back to the horses. Henry Marston was claiming it.

The hunters had to camp out again that night. Thel was worried about the horses left staked in the meadow, but when they returned to the main camp the following day he was relieved to find that only two horses had pulled their stakes. And they had stayed with the other horses and were easily caught.

The Marstons were only speaking to each other when it was necessary. In Thel's opinion the hunt was over. Besides the disasters that had befallen them, the season was closing in. October was well advanced. It was time to get these dudes out of the mountains.

Thel asked, "Do you still want to go to Mammoth, Mr. Marston?"

Marston chewed thoughtfully on a piece of elk steak. "I have decided it is not necessary. When we return to Boston I'll make a full report to the government. My attorney can forward it through our senator. However, if we run into some responsible soldiers I can give them my report. I have it all written down."

Thel said, "We'll break camp tomorrow and start for Montana. The Northern Pacific will have your railroad car by now."

"Hold on," said Marston. "I have only killed one elk. And what about the bison? Surely we're going to try for the bison?"

Thel had anticipated this. He said, "We'll move north and get out of Yellowstone Park. Once we're across the line into Montana, we shall find elk and maybe a buffalo."

The weather had moderated. Some of the snow had melted, easing the work. But with Ossie gone there was still more than enough for Thel and Tyghee. Eugene had begun helping but he was inexperienced. These delays, however, gave Henry Marston more time to hunt.

Thel discouraged him from killing big game in the park except what they needed for meat. But Marston was always riding off, then returning with waterfowl and a variety of smaller animals. The latter ranged from snowshoe hares through otters. The otters, he said, "would make a stole for Beatrice." Marston also killed beavers and porcupines to use as bait for wolves and coyotes. He was having a high old time for himself.

Once when his father and Tyghee were hunting, Eugene said to Thel, "He really enjoys killing, doesn't he? He needs to do it. There must be a connection between collecting as much money as possible and collecting animals the same way."

"I don't know much about money," said Thel. "But I've seen men that wanted to kill more than your dad. On some parties it takes two or three mules just to pack the ammunition. In the old days in Montana the ground was covered with elk and buffalo bones."

Thel was getting warmed up, "It wasn't just the whites, either. I've seen Indian girls whose best dresses had four hundred elk tusks hangin' on them."

Eugene said, "I didn't realize the Indians did such things."

Thel replied, "There's white men in these mountains today killin' elk for pelts and tusks. The Indians will trade a good pony for a few elk teeth."

Eugene remembered this later when the pack train wound down a long divide near the Montana border. In one meadow they counted the carcasses of twenty elk. All had been skinned and the tusks taken from the bulls' upper jaws.

"This is a filthy business," said Marston. "I thought this was stopped years ago."

"Now you see different," said Thel. "The only change is that there isn't near as much game as there used to be. And the fellows who do this work are mighty sneaky about it."

Despite the evident slaughter of elk by poachers, Thel was able to find a magnificent bull for Henry Marston. The evening Marston and his guide returned with this trophy Marston said to Eugene, "Look at these antlers. Instead of pottering around camp all day, do some hunting. It's the chance of a lifetime."

Eugene looked surprised. These were the first civil words he had heard from his father since the incident with the grizzly.

Eugene said, "No, thanks. I've had a good hunt. Unless we need meat I'll keep 'pottering'."

Eugene had been roaming the hills collecting arrowheads, spear points, and many other artifacts. Years later his collection of remnants from the vanished tribes would be gratefully accepted by a museum.

The next day Henry Marston said to Thel, "Eugene likes you. Take him hunting. I hate seeing him wandering these hills looking for old Indian junk."

Thel said, "I have asked him. Did you ever stop to think that he hasn't had a drink in weeks? I know he's craved one. He probably still does. Count it up as a plus that he's sober. It doesn't matter if he hunts or not."

Marston glared at Thel. "You may have a point—even if it isn't your business. But this trip has not done for Eugene what I hoped it would."

Thel recalled Eugene climbing the Teton and facing that wounded grizzly in the dark. Gene Marston might not be a prize, but Thel thought there was more to the young man than his father saw.

Thel dismounted and began examining some tracks. He needed a way of changing the subject.

"It's your buffalo, Mr. Marston. These tracks are old, but somewhere around here, if the poachers haven't beat you to him, there's a big bull buffalo."

"Splendid!" Marston clapped his gloved hands. "Riley, there will be a handsome bonus in this if I can take that buffalo."

What a rich man calls a "handsome bonus" is often much less than a poor guide lets himself expect. Thel had already learned this. And his heart was no longer in this hunting trip. But, almost in spite of himself, he went along.

The remainder of that day was spent trailing the bison. It was slow work. The ground was hard and storms had destroyed much of the old spoor. But Tyghee and Thel agreed that if they found a pattern in the bull's wandering they might shortcut and take him.

As they tracked, it was easier to find evidence of the hide hunters. Their tracks led to dozens of deer and elk carcasses. It appeared to be the work of two men. They worried Thel.

That night he said, "Gene, carry your rifle when you're out huntin' arrowheads. Hide hunters are mostly outlaw and they'd rob you in a minute."

Eugene protested, "That big rifle gets in my way when I'm hunting arrowheads."

Thel went into his tent and returned with the Colt revolver Eugene had given him. "Carry this. And keep your rifle in your saddle scabbard." Thel smiled. "Humor me."

Eugene Marston smiled in return and accepted the holstered revolver. Thel thought Eugene had come a long way from the mess at Threadlow's camp on the Gros Ventre.

October's golden days fell away like the yellow leaves on the aspen trees. The nights grew increasingly colder. After three fruitless days of following old buffalo tracks Thel was ready to quit. It had been snowing in the high country. The weather could close in on them at any time.

At supper Thel said to Marston, "Tyghee wants to go home. He's already stayed longer than we agreed. He wants to take his ponies and start south. He still has to make his own winter's meat."

"I thought the government fed Indians all winter," said Marston.

"Tyghee won't take it. He's an old-fashioned Shoshone," said Thel.

"Offer him more money," said Marston.

"I did." Thel threw out his hands, palms up. "Tyghee has enough money. Having more than he needs never occurs to him." Thel added, "You know there's some bad boys in this country. The three of us would be easy pickin's after Tyghee leaves."

"Come, come, Riley. You exaggerate. We haven't seen a soul. You said there were only two poachers on these jobs. Let's hunt one more day and see how we stand tomorrow night."

Thel agreed. Tyghee would stay one more day.

The country they hunted was rolling, sage-covered foothills. Scattered stands of juniper dotted the hills. There were countless brushy draws and ravines where a buffalo could feed in safety. The buffalo was wandering in a northeasterly direction, probably headed for the Missouri brakes. It was a frustrating search but, the tracks proved, the hunters were gaining on him.

At midday the group rested on a promontory and ate a cold lunch. Tyghee built a warming fire and Thel filled a pot from his canteen and made coffee. While the guides were busy Henry Marston studied the vastness before him with his field glasses.

"Hello," he said. "We have company."

Thel and Tyghee immediately looked in the direction Marston indicated. Thel uncased his own glasses.

"It's the Army," he said. "Eight riders."

In an hour the soldiers were within hailing distance. Some were dressed in Army blue and others wore shaggy buffalo coats. Thel waved and the troop turned in his direction. There were six weathered cavalrymen and two craven, dirty prisoners.

Sergeant Toone was in charge. "We've been out a week," he said. "These two gents have spent the season robbing camps and poaching game. We're takin' 'em to Mammoth for a hearing."

The two poachers, looking miserable and exhausted, stared at the ground. Thel found them typical. Border dregs who killed game for the pelts and left the meat to rot. Tent robbers who sneaked around and stole whatever they found. On the old frontier, scum like this often disappeared without explanation.

Thel said, "I guess it's their work we've been seein'. Maybe the elk will have a chance with these boys out of the country."

"That reminds me," said Henry Marston. "We had a run-in with some similar outlaws. I've written a full report of it. Please give it to your commanding officer." Marston handed a sealed envelope to the sergeant, who stuffed it inside his blouse. He and the sergeant then shook hands and the troop passed on.

When they had gone Marston said, "I'm relieved to have that settled. Now, Riley, you can't use those two as an excuse for quitting. We'll manage without Tyghee. Stay another week and there's an extra two hundred dollars for you!"

Thel nodded. He could not afford to refuse that much money.

Late that afternoon the men found even more to raise their spirits. There were now two buffalo. A second bull had joined the first one and the tracks were just two days old. Thel was optimistic. He urged Tyghee to stay and hunt.

The Indian refused. He would like to hunt buffalo again. If it were just for Thel he would stay. But the white hunter had a bad heart. He should not be allowed to kill the old father of the herds. Tyghee was going home.

In the morning he helped Thel and Eugene pack all the trophies and much of their equipment. Tyghee would detour, leaving the horses and baggage at Crow Agency. Thel and the Marstons could pick it all up later on their way to the Northern Pacific tracks.

Before Tyghee left, Thel paid him generously. He also gave him a large share of their remaining food and wished him a good winter. The two shook hands.

Thel said, "See you next fall, old friend."

Tyghee nodded and gripped his friend's shoulder. "Big hunt," he said. "Plenty game, make heap meat."

Then he was in the saddle and rounding up the pack animals. When the horses were moving before him, Tyghee turned and raised his arm.

"So long," said Thel, returning the salute.

Henry Marston was impatient to begin hunting. "We've lost the morning. Let's go."

"Be a couple more hours," said Thel. He explained that

they were moving camp closer to where they had seen the buffalo. "It'll save time in the long run," he explained.

Marston growled but he had no choice. Thel and Eugene packed the remainder of their outfit. By the time they had moved and pitched camp it was late afternoon.

But the day wasn't lost. Thel and the Marstons rode out and by sundown found the freshest tracks so far.

"This isn't more than a day old," said Thel. "If we don't find those bulls tomorrow, we'll get 'em next day sure."

Eugene did not want to shoot a buffalo. But he had never seen a live one in the wild, especially not two of the last old patriarchs left alive. He willingly joined the hunt. Although Eugene and his father scarcely spoke, they would ride together.

Thel still had eight horses. Before the morning's hunt he had to bring the spare animals in to water and then tie them in the junipers for the day. Eugene was becoming increasingly helpful. His father seldom lent a hand. Notwithstanding his efforts on the sheep hunt, H. B. Marston upheld the principle of keeping some distance between employer and employee.

A cold wind was blowing from the northwest as the men left camp. Thel looked into it. There was a pinkish light on the clouds. If he was any judge there would be snow by morning. He dreaded it but it would make the buffalo easier to track.

Without Tyghee the tracking was slower. The bulls had begun to travel faster. The men had to stay on their trail and move faster than the bison did.

By late afternoon the sky was streaked with dark clouds. Thel put in a silent request for tracking snow but not a blizzard. The ground had become hard and rocky. That slowed the tracking.

The buffalo had entered a coulee with good grass and water. When Thel found the bulls' beds he became excited. "Look, they were here last night." Looking around, he soon found the route the bulls had taken that morning.

CHAPTER SIXTEEN

THEL SAW THEM FIRST. THE BULLS WERE GRAZING ON AN open slope near a stand of juniper. They were huge, with massive withers and great shaggy heads. Each animal would weigh nearly a ton.

"Do you see 'em?" Thel asked.

"No. Where are they?" asked Marston, the excitement rising in his voice.

Thel quickly led Marston's eye to the buffalo. "They must be three miles away," said Marston.

"Yeah, too far for tonight. Shooting light is almost gone now."

Marston agreed and the trio returned to camp. En route Thel saw fresh horse tracks along their back trail. But it was dark and beginning to spit snow so he hurried on to camp.

At dinner the Marstons were both excited about the buffalo. Henry Marston had decided to use his heavy Winchester single-shot. "In memory of the vanished plainsmen," he said.

"You figurin' to kill 'em both?" asked Thel.

"I have a game room at my country place," replied Marston. "A buffalo head at each end of the room would be magnificent."

"What would you do with the meat?" asked Eugene.

"We could take some with us," said Marston. "The tongue and the hump are delicious."

Thel said, "Those bulls will dress out at better than a thousand pounds each. You'd be leavin' a ton of meat for the coyotes."

Marston considered this, then said, "We can't have that. Seen too much of that sort of thing already. What we'll do is send Riley back from the Crow Agency with horses and a working party. All the meat will be brought in and distributed to the Indians."

Thel admitted the scheme would work. He had just never before thought in terms of "cost is no object." He said, "We're still a long way from those buffalo. Let's turn in now and get an early start tomorrow."

They were all soon wrapped in their sougans. Thel was tired but he could not sleep. The horse tracks he had seen worried him. Could they have been made by strays? He liked knowing the answers to such questions. As he lay there in the darkness he heard a rustling against the tent canvas. It was snow beginning to fall in earnest.

Finally, Thel thought about Bea. He wondered if she were back in Philadelphia now. He had considered visiting her during the coming winter, but decided that would be foolish. Bea really wanted the big city and all the books and music folderol she and Marston had talked about. She probably wanted Marston. And Bea Woods was still pretty enough to get him. Thel rolled over and went to sleep.

Something awakened him. The horses were neighing and there was the muffled sound of movement outside the tent. Seizing his Winchester, Thel slid its muzzle out the tent flap.

The snow had stopped. It had been a moderate fall. The white blanket aided visibility. In the darkness Thel saw three loose horses wandering among the tethered stock. Dressing quickly, he went to investigate.

The loose horses snorted when Riley approached. But they did not run. They knew him. They were from the pack outfit Tyghee had left with nearly two days before.

Horses often got loose and came looking for old companions. Riley found some rope and prepared to catch the strays. Then he saw it. The remnants of a packsaddle were hanging under the belly of one of the horses. He caught this animal and removed what was left of the saddle. Somehow the animal's load had been lost and the saddle turned. The frightened horse had kicked the saddle into fragments.

It was unlike Tyghee to lose horses. But to have one escape from him with a loaded packsaddle was unthinkable. Calling to the Marstons to get up, Riley hurriedly began saddling their horses.

"What's the matter? It's still the middle of the night." Henry Marston stumbled from the tent still half asleep.

"Something's happened to Tyghee. These three horses came in a while ago. One still had the packsaddle hanging on." Thel did not stop working to explain. He said, "I can see OK. We'll backtrack these horses. I've got to find out what happened to Tyghee."

"But what about my buffalo?" asked Marston. "That Indian is fully capable of looking after himself."

Thel swung around to face Marston. It was all he could do to keep from hitting him. "Tyghee is in trouble. The buffalo aren't. Now get ready to ride."

Marston had never heard this tone in Riley's voice. Without another word he went to his tent. He reemerged almost immediately with Eugene. Both men were ready to ride.

The horse tracks were easy to follow in the snow. Knowing approximately where the animals had come from allowed Thel to take shortcuts. By daybreak he was five miles from camp and moving fast.

By midmorning they had found two more strays and were fifteen miles from camp. Beyond the foothills the snow had been light and melted shortly after sunup. Thel found Tyghee's tracks and followed them. They eventually led onto an open plain and around the base of a juniper-clad ridge. At the tip of this ridge something had happened. The packhorses had been scattered. Their tracks went off in all directions as if they had been suddenly frightened. There were boot tracks, too. It was all a jumble.

Thel looked around, then remounted his horse. He rode up the ridge to a rocky outcropping. From there he could see all around and command the plain below.

Someone else had been there. Thel knelt and picked up two fired .32 rimfire cartridges. How he had come to hate those pipsqueak rifles! Viro Pocket had had one. It was the same kind of weapon with which Ossie had tried to stop the charging grizzly. Now here it was again on this cold, windswept hill in Montana. About the only thing to be said for the .32 was that it did not make much noise.

Stuffing the spent cartridges into his pocket, Thel remounted and rode down to where the Marstons waited. "I think Tyghee's been ambushed," he said.

"Eugene found blood on the rocks over there," said Marston.

Without waiting to see if the Marstons were following, Thel began tracking. The packhorses had been gathered and driven away. Thel followed the trail at a trot. Within two miles he found where the horses had been driven into a patch of juniper. Here some of the horses had been caught and unpacked. Others, probably the skittish ones, had been shot. Packs and equipment lay scattered everywhere. The robbers had ransacked the baggage, taken what they felt was valuable, then fled.

Farther into the juniper several magpies were fluttering among the trees. Thel guessed what they had found.

Tyghee had been shot twice in the back. His killers had dumped his body behind some large rocks and thrown dirt and branches over it.

Picking up Tyghee in his arms, Thel carried him to a gnarled old tree. From the tree one could see both the sunrise and the sunset. Thel tenderly placed the Indian's body in the tree and tied it there with his lariat.

Then he turned to the Marstons. "I'm goin' after these boys. If you want to help, fine. If not, just head northeast. You'll hit Crow Agency in about twenty-five miles."

The Marstons spoke together, "We'll come."

Thel followed the trail until it was too dark to see. The men lay out that night, shivering in the bitter cold because Thel prohibited a fire. They ate jerky and moldy cheese salvaged from one of the packs. The men hardly spoke. Marston's teeth were chattering loudly enough to make Thel and Eugene nervous. To keep from freezing, the men walked in circles swinging their arms.

Lem Bischoff and Snub Freeney allowed themselves the luxury of a fire. They were hunched over it, roasting strips of meat.

"I don't think we got followed," said Feeney.

"Don't be so damned dumb. That stuff didn't belong to the Injun. Somebody's gonna be lookin' for it." Bischoff pulled his strip of meat from the skewer and cursed when he burned his lips.

He and Feeney knew the country and had no difficulty traveling at night. They had a dugout in some brakes ten miles to the northwest. Their plan was to go to the dugout, collect their hides and possessions, and make a dash for the Canadian border.

The men were leading six horses from Tyghee's string. Bischoff planned to use them for packing hides into Canada. There they would trade hides and horses to the Indians. The Canadian Sioux were dependable allies against the "Meri-cats." It was a simple plan but a good one. Bischoff had used it before. Still, he was taking no chances. He moved fast and watched his back trail.

At first light Thel saddled the horses and prepared to leave. Henry Marston asked him to wait.

"What's wrong?" Thel was impatient.

Marston said, "I've been thinking this over. We are making a mistake to rush after these bandits."

"I don't know how else we're gonna catch 'em," said Thel, swinging into the saddle.

"That's my point," Marston replied. "We need trained men, a posse, to capture these fellows. We're only three against two. They may have accomplices waiting ahead."

"If you're tellin' me you don't want to follow 'em, say it." Thel reined his horse around, eyeing Marston angrily.

"Eugene and I will go on to Crow Agency. The instant we arrive we will send you help. I'll pay generously. You just shadow these fellows until your help arrives."

Eugene was standing near his father. Thel looked inquiringly at him but Eugene looked away.

"I see how it is," said Thel. "At least do me one favor: go back to the camp and pack our stuff. Pack what was left in the junipers on the horses. A day's ride will see you in Crow Agency. You can leave my pay with the Army commander there. So long."

Thel started his horse. He wanted to gallop away from these treacherous snakes from Boston before he shot them both.

"Thel! Wait!" Eugene ran after him.

Thel pulled in his horse. Eugene came up and held out the Colt revolver with its holster and cartridge belt.

"Thanks." Thel buckled on the weapon and rode away. Never once did he look back at the Marstons. He despised them both. This was his last hunt.

As he rode he mentally savaged the Marstons. A few days ago Marston had been praising Tyghee for saving him from the grizzly. A few weeks ago he had boasted to Thel of his war record, saying he wanted Eugene to face danger. But now when danger was cunning and well armed, Marston weaseled. He was surprised at Eugene. The young man had appeared to be getting a grip on himself. Thel thought, "I was wrong about Bea, too."

Riley took the thieves' trail at a gallop. It was easy to follow. Thel raced recklessly for five miles before slowing his horse.

At noon he found where the killers had rested and cooked their meat. There was still warmth in the ashes of their fire.

As he did when tracking dangerous game, Thel moved off the killers' tracks. He followed a parallel course because he had to assume the men were watching their back trail. If they tried to ambush him he wasn't going to make it easy for them.

The outlaws' route was through wild, unsettled country. They made little effort to conceal their trail. Perhaps they felt time was on their side and the Canadian border was all the protection they needed.

By early afternoon Thel had calmed down. He realized that allowing the Marstons' treachery to dominate his thoughts wasted his own effectiveness. The men he was trailing were experienced and dangerous murderers.

Thel tried to keep to the higher ground. He watched the outlaws' trail from above and often tracked with his field glasses. His strategy was simple: see them before they saw him.

Lem Bischoff also had a pair of field glasses. At every vantage point he stopped and glassed the country behind them. He knew from the initials on some of the stolen gear that it was Thel Riley's party he'd robbed. It pleased him to get even with the drunken Easterner who had kneed him, but he was also fearful of Riley.

Riley's actual appearance alarmed him even more. Bischoff spotted Thel in patchy timber below some rimrock. The rider was too far away to be positive about. But anyone else would not be staying off the back trail and trying to come in on them from the side. Bischoff signaled Feeney to stop. The horses were quickly hidden in a thicket.

"What'll we do?" Snub Feeney was wide-eyed with fear. Bischoff jerked Snub's .32 single-shot from its scabbard and thrust it into his hands. "Here. He hasn't seen us. We're gonna bust him."

Bischoff's plan was murderously simple. Feeney would go back down the trail to a rocky outcropping and hide there. Lem Bischoff was going up a draw that cut the slope where Riley was riding. The draw would conceal Bischoff until he too was in position. They would have Riley in a cross fire.

When Riley was in range Bischoff would shoot him with his heavy rifle. That should end it. But if it did not, Snub could pin Thel down until Bischoff moved in and finished the job.

"That dude-pusher hasn't a chance—unless we give him one." Bischoff gave Feeney a pat on the back as the two separated.

Inside, Bischoff wasn't so sure. He was going to feel much safer once he got a bullet into Riley. Bischoff was carrying a heavy Sharps rifle. With it he had killed literally thousands of deer, elk and buffalo. He had also killed men. He knew his Sharps as well as any man could know a weapon.

After he had climbed the draw and crept into position behind some rocks, Lem raised the rifle's rear sight. The Sharps was cocked and ready to fire. Bischoff took a careful rest with his rifle and waited.

He did not have long to wait. Thel soon appeared. But he was still out of sure range. Bischoff aligned his sights on Thel's chest and waited.

Just as a watched wild animal senses danger and becomes uneasy, Thel began feeling apprehensive. He stopped beside a large serviceberry bush. Raising his field glasses he carefully studied the area ahead. Finding nothing, he clucked to his horse and moved forward.

As Thel advanced, Bischoff's finger tightened on his trigger. He could hold dead on now and Riley would be finished when he hit the ground.

Preparing to fire, Bischoff adjusted his rifle ever so slightly. There was the briefest flash as the sunlight struck his gun barrel. Thel saw it and instinctively jerked back on his reins.

His horse, Tom, threw up his head and as he did Bischoff's bullet struck him squarely on the nose. The heavy slug ripped through bone and tissue to lodge in the horse's brain. He dropped so fast that Riley just managed to kick his feet clear of the stirrups. As Thel struck the ground he was stung by flying fragments of lead and rock. Snub Feeney's .32 bullet had barely missed him. Thel pressed himself flat beside the body of his dead horse. His hands groped blindly for the butt of his Winchester.

In that instant Thel was gripped by panic. His horse had fallen on the rifle. It was buried under a thousand pounds of dead weight. Riley froze. Then he felt for the Colt on his belt. When he gripped its butt the moment of panic left him.

He lay still, his panic replaced by a mixture of fear and anger. He collected his thoughts. Thel had not heard the shot that killed his horse. But he heard the "boom" of Bischoff's next round and the sickening "thump" as the slug slammed into the horse's carcass. Thel was so tightly pinned that he dared not so much as raise his head.

His mind raced. "They don't know I lost my rifle. They'll be careful." As he lay there Thel was peppered by more flying bits of rock and lead from Snub Feeney's rifle.

"Snub!" Bischoff yelled. "Take it easy. Did I hit him?"

"Couldn't tell for sure. He ain't movin'." Despite Bischoff's warning, Snub Feeney popped up to send another shot in Thel's direction.

Using Feeney's name was a mistake. Thel now knew who his attackers were. He also knew that Bischoff carried a big single-shot and Feeney a .32 single-shot. A plan began to form in his mind.

He had learned to respect Feeney's .32. But he did not respect Feeney. Thel waited until Bischoff's next shot ripped into the horse. Then, staying as flat as he could, he rolled and wriggled around behind the horse's rump. For his pains he took a bullet from Feeney that tore a furrow across the calf of his leg.

"He moved, Lem! I seen him!" Feeney fairly shrieked.

Thel's move still kept the horse between himself and Bischoff. But he could now look down and see the rocks where Feeney was hiding. They were one hundred yards away and far beyond the accurate range of a .45 Colt. But they were well within its killing range. Thel fired a shot and saw it strike several feet short of Feeney's position.

For his effort he received a volley from the two bandits. Bischoff's bullet buzzed scant inches above his head. The man was a dead shot. But Feeney had been frightened. He simply held his rifle up above the rocks and, without aiming, fired in Thel's direction. Thel returned the fire, sending his next bullet into the rocks beside Feeney. Like an artilleryman, he was getting the range.

Thel could not help grinning when Feeney yelped. The bullet had not come within four feet of the little man but its effect was almost as good as if he'd hit him. Thel cranked off two more shots but Feeney, cowering in his hideout, didn't reply.

Bischoff did. His next bullet thudded into the horse, stopping just inches from Thel. If he kept that up the horse would be pounded into hamburger. Thel knew that a bullet can penetrate hamburger more easily than compact bone and muscle.

The shock of being grazed by Feeney's bullet began to wear off. Thel craned to look at his throbbing leg. It was oozing blood. He flexed his toes. He was not badly hurt.

Lem Bischoff did not know that. He lowered his head and rested it on his arm, thinking. There were six cartridges lying on the rock in front of him. He searched through his pockets and found two more. He guessed Feeney had about the same amount of ammunition.

So, when he saw the little man raise his rifle up over the rocks and fire without aiming, he was furious. "Snub! You damn yellowbelly, make those shots count!" For emphasis he planted a Sharps slug near Feeney's head. He called, "Now shoot to kill or I'll kill you!"

Bischoff watched as Snub prepared for another shot. His movements were so slow that they were barely perceptible. But Snub did at least give the appearance of aiming. The aim and the shot came so fast that it was a credit to Thel that he had time to return the fire. His bullet went wide but Snub cringed and cowered behind the rocks all the same.

Shaking his head in disgust, Bischoff gathered up his remaining cartridges and slid back into the draw. He was going to do what Thel had dreaded. Bischoff was moving up the draw and into a commanding position above Thel. From there he could look down and kill Riley as easily as killing a rabbit in his hole.

Thel was so tightly pinned that he dared not move to check on Bischoff. The silence was ominous. Thel studied the terrain around him. There was no shelter within twenty yards.

Riley knew that at any second he would be a dead man. It fired his anger to imagine himself just lying there and letting the likes of Lem Bischoff kill him. He saw Snub looking up the hill. He too must be wondering what Bischoff was doing.

Feeney did not realize Thel saw him. Only the upper part of his head was exposed between a cleft in the rocks.

Instantly Thel extended the Colt, holding it in both hands. He put the blade of the front sight on Feeney's head, then raised the barrel to allow for the range. Sweat beaded on Thel's forehead as he concentrated on making an almost impossible shot. He fired.

"Damn!" Thel had come so close; just an inch to the left and Snub Feeney's brains would have been scrambled. Riley's fury exploded. He glanced up the slope and caught a glimpse of Bischoff getting into position. The man was two hundred yards away. But Thel, still holding the Colt in both hands, fired at him anyway.

Bischoff heard the slug buzz harmlessly overhead. Nevertheless he ducked and went scrabbling on his hands and knees for cover.

"Snub!" he cried. "He's clear, take him!"

But Snub did not fire and Thel dived back behind the dead horse. He had decided to risk exposing himself to Feeney in order to keep the horse between himself and Bischoff.

Thel looked up at the sky. It was blue with fleecy white clouds drifting overhead. Sunshine streamed through the breaks in the clouds and warmed the surface of the earth. It shone on Thel Riley, but he did not feel it. The chill of death crept over him. And he hated it.

"I'm going to run. Maybe I can make those trees." He was talking to himself. He pulled his legs under him and prepared to run. He was fighting off the fate Bischoff planned for him.

What Thel did not know was that while his last shot at Snub Feeney missed, it had taken effect. The heavy .45 bullet had broken off a sharp fragment of stone. The chip hit Snub Feeney in the left eye. He fell to the ground clutching his face and crying with pain. The wound, while not fatal, was all it took to put a man like Feeney out of a gun battle.

Thel bounced to his feet and began running. His leg hurt and he knew he was too slow. He had only taken three strides when a shot rang out. Thel dived, hit rolling, then got up and started running again. He thought, "How in hell did he miss me?" Thel ran for the trees. When he reached them he whooped in amazement. He was still alive!

Eugene Marston lay on top of the rimrock and looked down at Lem Bischoff's body sprawled on the ridge below. Then he stood up and flipped the lever of his Winchester. The spent cartridge clattered among the rocks at his feet. Holding his rifle in one hand, he raised his arms and waved.

"Thel! Don't shoot! It's me, Gene Marston!"

A few minutes later the two men were standing together. Snub Feeney, his head half hidden in a bandanna, sat at their feet. Feeney was rocking back and forth on his haunches and moaning.

Thel picked up Snub's rifle. It was a battered .32 single-shot. The rifle that had killed Tyghee. For a moment Thel stood poised, deliberating whether or not to swing the rifle down and smash Snub's skull.

"Wait!" Eugene stepped forward and grasped the rifle. "Look," he said, pointing to the .32's butt stock. There, crudely burned with a red-hot nail, was the name "V. Pocket."

"It's the sheepherder's gun!" Eugene exclaimed.

Thel reached down and dragged Feeney to his feet. "You did it! You and Lem Bischoff killed that sheepherder!"

The man cowered and held up his hands to ward off a blow. "Lem done it! I didn't think we was gonna hurt the bugger. But Lem hit him too hard. We knifed him to make it look like the Injuns done it." Feeney started to blubber and Thel shoved him back down on the ground.

"So your old man killed those Indians by mistake. I

wondered why they didn't have anything of Pocket's." Thel sat down and looked at Eugene. "Where's your dad now?"

"He'll be at the Crow Agency waiting for us," Eugene replied. "After you left I realized I had to come, too."

"I'm sure glad you did," said Thel. "Which one of us is going to tell your old man he's a murderer?"

"I can't do it," said Eugene. "But I want to be there when you tell him."

About the Author

FRANK CALKINS has been a magazine editor, a news-paper columnist, a big-game hunting guide, and a Utah state game warden. He is the author of two nonfiction books, ROCKY MOUNTAIN WARDEN and JACKSON HOLE. Ballantine published his most recent Western novel THE LONG RIDERS' WINTER in 1985. He lives on a five-acre enclave in a national wildlife refuge in Wyoming.

A round-up of BALLANTINE'S best... **W**esterns by your favorite authors

By the year 2000, 2 out of 3 Americans could be illiterate.

It's true.

Today, 75 million adults...about one American in three, can't read adequately. And by the year 2000, U.S. News & World Report envisions an America with a literacy rate of only 30%.

Before that America comes to be, you can stop it...by joining the fight against illiteracy today.

Call the Coalition for Literacy at toll-free **1-800-228-8813** and volunteer.

Volunteer Against Illiteracy. The only degree you need is a degree of caring.

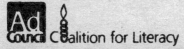

Ad Council   Coalition for Literacy   LV-2